BILLIONAIRE COWBOY AUCTIONED AT CHRISTMAS

Billionaire Cowboys of True Love, Texas,
Book Four

HOPE
MOORE

Billionaire Cowboy Auctioned at Christmas

Billionaire cowboy Jake Tanner has no plans to get married anytime soon and although he caught a garter at a wedding recently makes him even more determined to prove to his brothers that them falling in love with the first woman they saw after catching a garter is just a coincidence. Besides, he ran into the local veterinarian after catching the garter and she and him are like vinegar and water...they already found out they don't mix.

When one of his brothers signs him up for the True Love Texas Christmas Bachelor Auction he's a good sport and agrees. A home-cooked meal in exchange for decorating the winning bidder's house for Christmas sounds like a good trade. Especially since the money raised always goes for a good cause.

Veterinarian Hanna Cork needs to invest in her new community. She's just bought an old farm on the outskirts of True Love and a little help putting up Christmas lights would be nice, so bidding on a cowboy sounds like the perfect plan. However, the cocky, gorgeous Jake Tanner, whom she dated briefly, is the last man she would bid on...until someone else bids on him and to her horror she can't stop herself from bidding against every other female who wants him.

Now that she's won him what is she supposed to do with him?

And how is she going to convince him that her bidding on him has absolutely nothing to do with being attracted to him?

This unusually snowy Christmas in True Love Texas is promising to be one for the record books as Jake and Hanna find out that falling in love often comes unexpectedly.

CHAPTER ONE

Jake Tanner stared at the garter he had just caught. He almost hadn't come to this wedding since he knew everyone in the building was watching to see if he caught the garter. And now, here he stood holding it, despite being determined not to.

And when he looked around, everybody was grinning at him.

Including his older brother Cole. Jake frowned at him and had a bad feeling he knew where Cole's thoughts were, along with many of the people in the room who had been keeping up with what happened when one of the Tanner men caught a garter.

"Don't say it," he warned.

Cole laughed. "It looks like you'll be getting married pretty soon."

"Nope, not true. Just because you, Bret, and Levi have gotten married after catching a garter doesn't mean I'm going to. And Austin isn't looking for tying himself down yet either. I'm glad y'all are all happy, but I'm not ready. I see your wife coming this way. Tell her I said hello, but I've got to leave." And with that he spun and headed toward the door—but immediately ran hard into Hanna Cork.

She wobbled and he dropped the garter, which he didn't mind at all, and grabbed her arms to steady her. "Sorry about that." He stared into her pretty face. She was the veterinarian of True Love, and they'd dated a few times not long after she'd taken the job a little over a year ago.

She met his gaze. "Sorry, I was looking over my shoulder saying hello to someone. You can let go of me."

He hadn't even realized he was still holding on to her. He dropped his hands. "Okay, glad you didn't fall. I'm heading out.""Yes, well, you might want to pick up your garter that you just dropped."

He frowned. "I guess I'll pick it up, but that

doesn't mean anything."

"Believe me, I know. Anyway, head on out." She stepped around him and started walking off.

Aggravating as it was to him, he turned to watch her and found that she was looking over her shoulder at him too.

"Have fun. I'm sure you're really busy right now."

Pausing, she turned back to him. "I actually am. So busy that I haven't even had time to think about Christmas. It's coming up in three weeks and I haven't even gotten my tree up, haven't gotten a light on the exterior of my house. It isn't the most important thing, but I don't know why I'm talking to you about that. See you later." And then she walked off, disappearing into the crowd.

He stood there completely irritated at her determination to get out of his presence. They had dated briefly, very briefly, two times to be exact, not long after she'd opened her clinic in True Love. She'd said no to a third date and that she didn't think they were a good match and they hadn't seen each other often since then. He'd made sure of it, letting his brothers handle all emergency calls with her. Then when his brother Levi had taken in an abandoned, very sick horse for the sheriff's office and Jake had been out there helping taking care of the injured animal when she'd come out to help. It had been awkward.

Now only since she had started seeing his brother's injured horse that he had brought in had he spoken to her, and that had been a little while ago. But the weird thing was since speaking with her, he had thought about her more. To the point of driving him a little bit crazy. But that was ridiculous. She had made it clear she had no interest in him. Or if she had a little interest, she was *not* interested in it.

He turned and headed back out the door. He had a lot going on in his life and he was still shocked by all of his brothers who had gotten married over the last few months. It was fairly amazing how they each caught a garter, but he looked down at the one he held in his hands—he wasn't getting married because of a piece of material.

Or the lore that you are supposed to marry the first person you meet after you catch a garter! He could tell anybody who asked him about it that marriage wouldn't be between him and the local vet, Hanna Cork.

Hanna's nerves were a bit shaken after running into Jake. She hurried behind the cake table where she was supposed to help pass out the cake in just a few moments. She needed to be calm and not thinking about him, but she could not get the gorgeous cowboy off her mind.

They had dated early on when she had moved here. Even though she'd heard things about him that had told her he wasn't a man she was interested in dating. Why she'd agreed had been a mistake. He was not the kind of guy, she realized during the second date, who was interested in marrying, which was the reason she was dating.

He was gorgeous, entertaining, fun. But he wasn't someone she wanted to eventually marry, which was the only kind of guy she wanted to date. And why she hardly dated anyone. She wanted a man who was serious, took building a family seriously, and who wasn't always just thinking about ranching and having a good time. She knew he ranched well and had been attracted to him the moment she'd first seen him, despite having heard he dated a lot and loved having a good time. And she'd heard that from high school on he had been an entertaining man. Then after his family had become billionaires by hitting all kinds of oil on their huge ranch, he had been on the front of many tabloids.

She was highly attracted to him despite this but knew by the second date that she had to stop dating him. He'd been fun and flirted with her and made her feel extremely attracted to him. But she knew a man like him, with the past that he had, that she wasn't looking to marry a man who obviously loved a dating life.

She lived a quiet life when not doctoring on animals, and she wanted to marry a man who would also enjoy a quiet life and wanted a family. She feared, despite how attracted she was to him that he was not the man for her.

"You made it just in time," her friend Natalie said. "Here comes the bride and groom, and after their picture we start slicing."

She looked at her friend. "Sorry, I got a little held up back there."

"I saw that gorgeous Jake Tanner keep you from falling. I wish he would hold me up."

"Natalie, sometimes what you wish for isn't the best thing."

They moved out to the side to make sure they weren't in the way as the couple cut their cake while their picture was taken. When they were finished, she and Natalie took their places and started slicing the beautiful cake.

Natalie leaned close. "So, you said sometimes what you wish for isn't the best thing. My question for you is, did you wish for Jake? I noticed y'all went out a while back."

"You need to let this go, okay. We went out a few times, and I stopped dating him. I'm looking for a man who wants a family. His actions clearly say differently." She gave her a warning look then turned to the people waiting for cake. "Please, take what you want. I hear it's delicious."

She stayed busy and thank goodness Natalie said nothing else about Jake, which was good because she needed to stop thinking about him.

CHAPTER TWO

The morning after the wedding Jake parked his truck in True Love—this was the strangest named town, but he had lived here all his life and he still wasn't used to it. Whenever he went to other places, people teased him about the name when he told them where he was from. Sometimes he wanted to name a different town, but he didn't. This morning the town was decorated for Christmas and very pretty. There were wreaths on all the shop's doors, and somebody had put out pots of red Poinsettias. He saw that down the street there was a really cute group of metal reindeers, and further down the road in front of the church, he'd noticed as he'd passed that there was a very nice manger scene. True Love enjoyed decorating for Christmas. They had always had things going on in December and next Friday night, three weeks before Christmas, they were having the town Christmas party. And the town was ready.

He entered the feed store just as his friend Max, who was the head of the party committee this year, spotted him.

"Hey buddy, I'm glad I ran into you," Max said. "Come out here, I've got something to ask you." He walked out the door, totally expecting Jake to follow him.

Jake did as his friend asked and followed him outside. "What's up? How is the party planning going? I still can't believe you volunteered for that."

Max gave him a funny look. "Well I can't either, I have to tell you it's been a little bit of a chore this year. I didn't realize how many opinions these ladies have about what they want to go on at these parties. And well, this year, even though I tried to talk them out of it, they decided on having a giveaway at the party."

"That's not new. They always have some kind of giveaway."

"Yeah, but it has been a long time since they gave away a bunch of cowboys."

"Cowboys?"

"Yep. And the look on your face is the look I probably had when they told me that was what they wanted to do. They've insisted on it, so here we are at the end of the week getting the men in order. And the ladies think you would be a great giveaway. Now don't look at me like that…"

Oh, he was looking at him alright, with a stop right there, glare. But Max didn't stop.

"They asked me to ask you and I was actually going to call you later today, but we ran into each other here. So the deal is, you have to get up there and anybody who wants to fix you supper and have you decorate their house and maybe their Christmas tree for Christmas, you're to help them. And they feed you supper or lunch. Everybody knows that you can hang lights on houses since you have helped some of them before. They also know that you're wealthy and single and that this would be them buying a date with you. Meaning everyone feels like you will be a very popular bid."

"Look, I don't mind helping someone decorate their house if they need me too. But the idea of standing up in front and have women bidding on me… Well, I don't really like the idea of thinking about having somebody buying me."

"I know you don't but honestly, you'd be a huge help to me by doing this."

His friend had helped him out a lot of times growing up. Staring at him now, he wanted to just go get in his truck and drive away, wanted to tell Max no, but he couldn't. "Okay, I'll do it. I can't believe I came to get some dog food and I ended up being the dog food."

Max laughed. "Well, all I can say is that you never know how things work out. And who knows, you may enjoy being the dog food."

"Oh no, I can tell you it won't be for long. I can decorate fast."

Hanna walked into the Civic Center, where they were decorating for the Christmas party happening that

Friday night. She was hoping it would be a great success and had offered to help decorate if she wasn't on an emergency call.

"Welcome, Hanna," Ellie Tanner greeted her from the decorating table.

Across the table from her were her two sisters-in-law, Tulip and Rita. They were all really nice, and she enjoyed them when she was around them.

"Hey, good to see all of you here," she said, smiling brightly.

Rita patted the table. "Come join us. We're making candy bowls for the tables."

"As if we all need a lot of candy." Tulip laughed.

"Well, I like it," Rita said. "How about you, are you a candy fan, Hanna?"

She grinned. "I do like candy. My only problem with helping fill those containers with candy is I will want to eat it all."

They all laughed, and Ellie handed her a piece of candy. A chocolate one covered in a silver wrapper. Yup, it was a danger zone. She set her purse under the table and got to helping them.

After a minute, Tulip paused and looked at her. "You know, you are the perfect person to do our giveaway." She looked at her sisters-in-law and suddenly they were grinning at her.

Rita reached out and grabbed her arm. "You are, because I noticed when I passed by your house this week that you don't have anything decorated. And I know you are an extremely busy gal being a veterinarian. So that makes you the perfect type bidder."

"Bidder for what?"

"We need you to participate because you are one of the single ladies who needs this. You don't date much, and your house is not decorated, and I know that you have been so busy that you could use some help decorating. We'd like you to make some bids on at least one of the cowboys who will be auctioned off. You may not win him, but your bid will help the bids go up and that will be a huge help raising money."

"Bidding on a cowboy?"

Rita nodded. "Yes. There will be about six cowboys that you know, local guys who are going to be auctioned off. Their job is to put up whatever you need on the outside of your house to decorate for Christmas. The job is Saturday and he can help you get your Christmas tree inside if you need it or put up the outside lights. Whatever you need, that's his job and then you will feed him. How does that sound?"

Hanna's eyes narrowed as she looked at the three ladies staring at her. "Well, I guess that's a really good idea. I have had no time to get any decorating done so that would actually be kind of cool if I had an afternoon to get it done before Christmas. I mean, after the thing this weekend, there will only be two weeks left. I was wondering if I should even decorate this late."

"You should decorate just because it will help your spirits," Tulip said, smiling encouragement.

"Please do a little bidding," Rita said. "You know the money is going to go and help someone."

Tulip got a serious expression. "Don't forget, if you see somebody up there who appeals to you for dating, then bid as long as it takes to win him. It will be a great way to spend some time with him. If nobody appeals to you then just bid on one of them to come out and help you. The money is a donation and a great thing."

"You know," Rita said, slowly. "They talked Jake into getting auctioned off, and I saw you two run into each other at the wedding the other night."

Hanna frowned as her stomach tightened. "Jake and I don't really get along. You know we went out, and he's just not the kind of guy I want to date. If I date someone it's because I'm looking for a potential partner—a husband, and he and I just didn't match on that. We realized that."

"Really? Why is that," Tulip asked.

The other two ladies were looking at her with questions in their eyes. "When I marry, I want a man who is focused on us and our future family and our home. Jake's focused on a lot of other things. We just don't really get along."

The sisters-in-law looked at each other.

Tulip smiled at her. "Well that's fine but we're just saying if you see anybody up there you want to spend some money on, please do. We assumed with as busy as you've been this year that you might have some extra money, you could donate for a good cause. It's going through the fire department's donation fund and tax-deductible. And so, if you need an end of the year tax–deduction, this would be a good cause.I think it is, because it's going to be given to someone in need. So then, just give a bid because giving a bid doesn't mean you're going to win it, but there you go. And it does not have to be my brother-in-law. But to me, you two seem like a perfect couple."

Hanna's eyes narrowed and her lips dropped into a frown. "Why do you say that?"

Tulip smiled big. "Because you are both interested in animals, you both like the outdoors and… well we've all seen the way y'all look at each other. Y'all aren't around each other a lot, but I've seen the look and I think you might be in denial."

Hanna coughed. "Believe me, there is no denial. Anyway, can we change the subject?"

The gals all chuckled and she was fairly certain they were getting tickled at her because they believed she was in denial about the one guy who really got her nerves and pulse riled up.

Were they right?

CHAPTER THREE

Jake walked into the main barn at the family's ranch. His brothers were all standing over in the corner area where the coffee pot sat on a bar beside a refrigerator. All their life they had used the coffee pot in the house's kitchen, but then Cole had gotten married and they'd moved their morning meeting spot here in the barn. They didn't really want to go in the house this early and disturb Tulip's morning. When they'd come up with the coffee pot in the barn, they'd liked it a lot.

Cole held up the coffee pot and started pouring some coffee in a mug. "I'm sure you need this this morning."

"Yeah, a big one."

Cole poured the coffee. "Are you upset because you caught that garter?"

Levi smiled. "Cole told us you didn't have a happy look on your face after you caught it. And then you left right afterward. Were you running?"

"No." He gave Levi a lay-off-the-teasing glare.

"That's what we heard," Bret said, chuckling.

Only Cole had been at that wedding and he had hoped they hadn't heard he had caught a garter, but he'd suspected Cole would tell them.

His brother Austin, the doctor, hadn't said anything yet. He was leaning against the counter sipping his coffee. With his dress shirt and his well-starched jeans, he was probably heading to the hospital. "Cole said he saw you talking with Hanna Cork on your way out the door."

"Just a very few moments." He had feared they'd hear about him running into Hanna.

Austin's grin widened. "I also heard you're going to be in the Christmas giveaway. Going to have a herd of ladies bidding on spending time with you."

"Sounds like we are going to have some

entertainment watching your wedding romance start." Cole grinned.

Enough. "Okay, guys, yes, it was a strange evening last night. And yes, I caught the garter, but it doesn't mean anything. I'm not ready to get married. I know y'all thought you weren't ready when y'all caught a garter, but you obviously were. I'm not, so it doesn't matter if I caught a garter or didn't."

His brothers all stared at him with grins.

Austin spoke, "Obviously I haven't caught a garter so I'm still standing over here with nothing hanging over my head. I'll be anxious to see what happens to you because if you end up getting married, I probably won't end up going to another wedding. If I do have to go to one, I'll stay away from that pile of men waiting to catch a garter. Even if it happened to be your wedding and you wanted me to stand in the line."

Jake laughed despite not being thrilled by the conversation. "Believe me, if that were the case, I wouldn't blame you."

"You know it's terrible how you make getting married sound hideous," Levi said. "It's the best thing that can happen to you. I promise you the day I married Rita has been the best day of my life. Along with gaining Toby as my son."

"Same for me and Ellie," Bret added.

"Exactly my feelings about finding Tulip after catching a garter," Cole agreed.

"I have no vote in that," Austin said, his lips curling slightly.

"Well, look guys, it's obvious to tell that y'all are happy but I'm just not ready. I decided a while ago that going out on a casual date is what I enjoy. I like being only responsible for me. And after we first struck oil out here on the ranch and the tabloids went crazy with their stories on us dating, me in particular, well, I learned my lesson. I was young and did do a few dates that I might not have done, but the crazy tabloids made them far wilder than they were and made me sound like a rich wildcat. And then they threw out full blown lies too. It made me just stop dating for a long while, until they lost interest for the most part, thank goodness."

"Believe me," Austin said. "I watched what they

did to you and it kept me hard at work to graduate medical school. And then continue on two years since I graduated and started at the hospital. You did get abused by them."

"Yeah, you've practically not dated at all. Wish I'd learned from you. But now I stick around here and help out in town when needed. I smile at weddings but I'm not looking to do it myself. I enjoy life right now. I like our work here on the ranch, there's a lot to do and I enjoy it. So as far as I'm concerned, you guys can get married and have all the babies and I'll just be a good uncle. And as far as me putting decorations up for somebody over the weekend, well, I can do nice things without falling in love."

His brothers all laughed, making him uncertain if they agreed with him or were laughing at him thinking he was the one in control of his love life.

Bret studied him. "Well, maybe when you do fall in love it will just strike you like a lightning bolt. Speaking of who you ran into right after you caught the garter."

He grimaced, knowing his brothers had all been

curious about why he and Hanna had only dated twice. They all knew that he and Hanna avoided each other since they'd dated. They were all grinning at him and he knew what they were thinking. "Alright guys, again, I'm telling you not to get any ideas. She and I just didn't work out. Me catching a garter and running into her doesn't change that."

"The way I see it," Austin said, sending a look at him and then his brothers. "If it's meant to be, it will happen. One thing is for sure, we'll have a good time watching to see what happens." He winked at Jake.

"Yes, we will," Bret agreed.

And Cole and Levi did also.

Jake needed to get out of there. "Well, guys, I hope you're not expecting too much entertainment because you're going to be highly, highly disappointed." And then he set his coffee down and headed for his truck.

On Friday night Hanna walked into the Christmas party, her stomach rocking slightly. She was running late because she'd had a very busy day. She had thought there was a possibility that work would keep her from attending the party. Which at this point, thinking about going to a party where Jake Tanner was being auctioned off was a little unnerving. Why she really didn't know, but she had been bothered ever since the girls had told her that's what was going to happen.

The town party was busy as it always was, but this year it was busier, and she suspected since they were auctioning off cowboys, more women had come. More single women. Of course, it could be her imagination, but it seemed like more women were here. She took her coat off and hung it in the coatroom, which was not too far from the door. When she walked back out, she saw her friend waving at her to cross the room. She headed toward her, saying hello to people on the way.

Natalie grabbed her arm. "Finally. You were worrying me. I was beginning to think you were not going to make it."

"I had the same worry but I'm just thirty minutes late and the party goes on for hours." She gave her friend a frown. "Is there something wrong?"

"No, I just wanted to make sure you were here for when they started the auction."

She had talked to Natalie about being asked to bid on a cowboy. Her friend had known they were going to ask her and had been excited about it. "I'm okay, just busy at work. I promised everyone I would make a bid, so I'm glad I made it in time to fulfill my promise."

"Me too. I was worried you might not get here in time. Look over there." She nodded toward the edge of the crowd.

Hanna looked the direction Natalie indicated and there stood Jake. Her heart instantly began to beat rapidly. He was gorgeous tonight. He wore a red western shirt, starched jeans, and a black cowboy hat, in which all was a compliment to his handsome face. "I see him."

Natalie took hold of her arm. "I think you should bid on him. I know you say there's nothing between the two of you, but I know y'all dated. I know it was for just a couple of times, and I'm always confused why you stopped that soon. I've seen y'all speak sometimes, and yes, you seem kind of stiff and nervous, but you always make me wonder if there's more beneath all that reaction."

She took Natalie's arm and pulled her back behind some other people so Jake wouldn't see them. "Look, I will bid on whoever I get the drive to bid on, but I cannot guarantee that I will bid on him. He really is not my match and I just don't understand why I would do that."

Natalie frowned at her. "Okay, it's your call but you know how I feel. I just think it would be a good idea. If you win somebody, are you prepared to decorate tomorrow? You'll have two weekends before Santa comes, so at least your decorating will be done a little before Christmas."

"It would be great. I would have my stuff done, but more than likely if I don't win, I'm not going to decorate. It's just too much work for just me."

"I know that's why I'm saying bid to where you win somebody, and it will be done tomorrow."

She hadn't decorated for years after her dad died, but then she started decorating again in memory of him, and she hadn't been able to stop. But this year was not the year, with all these animals who were tending to have problems like crazy, she was just too tired. She had been praying that maybe over the holiday, things would slow down and they had a little yesterday. But today she'd been late for the party and now she realized she might get a cowboy who could decorate her own house tomorrow.

"Thank you for all this worry for me, and you know that you're very special to me. I'm very grateful to have you as a friend."

Natalie hugged her. "And I am very grateful for having you as a friend. The day you showed up in town as our veterinarian was just a great day. I want you to find a partner and be happy like you deserve."

"Thanks, but it's not happening tonight. Or tomorrow. If I bid, it's purely to help out."

CHAPTER FOUR

Jake took a drink of his punch and glanced to the left just in time to see Hanna and Natalie disappearing behind a group of guests. He caught a glimpse of her pretty red dress and instantly thought of a Christmas present—not exactly the way he wanted to see her. As she disappeared, he also glimpsed her pretty legs.

Why was he looking at her legs?

Gee, ever since he'd run into her at the wedding, after he had caught the garter, and then said yes to this auction he just kept getting weird thoughts.

He turned his back, hoping to get her out of his brain.

"You look worried." Bret studied him.

He hitched a brow. "Maybe you can bid on me when I go up there. Then somebody who might really need help, or someone willing to pay a lot to help the charity, would bid on me. It is for *charity*."

"It would be kind of wrong for me to bid."

Jake sighed. "I'll represent the Tanners on my own then. See if Austin hadn't been booked to work tonight, which could have been on purpose, I could have talked him into being up here beside me. He would be very helpful in raising money, I'm sure."

Bret laughed. "Yeah, you know he was our main worker at the ranch before he set his mind on being a doctor. Then we had to fill in for him."

They both laughed because Austin had grown up working hard on the ranch but since he had become an emergency room doctor, he loved to help on the ranch when he could, but it wasn't much.

"You'll do fine, I'm certain," Bret encouraged.

Some of their friends came up to talk and they started into a deep conversation about what they were all doing for Christmas.

One of the single ranchers they knew looked at

him and grinned. "I hear you're going to be up there. Me too. I'm hoping somebody worth dating will think enough of me to bid on me. This could be a really cool way to meet a wife. I mean future wife."

"Oh yeah, I don't want anybody's wife bidding on me," Jake said, laughing along with all the guys in the group.

"I said that wrong obviously."

"Obviously. Hope you get what you want." Jake decided he needed something to drink and some distance, so he excused himself and walked over to the refreshment line. He got his punch and started walking away when Hanna emerged from the crowd. Once again, she was looking backward. He held his drink out of the way as she ran into him once again.

Hanna gasped, staring at Jake. "Not again. What is my problem? I'm sorry. I don't run into people often and it's been you twice in less than a week." It was last Saturday she'd ran into him and tonight it was only Friday.

He smiled. "Well, I have to say at least I've been lucky enough to be watching and able to keep you from falling."

She took a deep breath. "Thank you. I hear you're going to be auctioned off to put lights on the winner's home."

"Right. They talked me into it. But thankfully I like decorating and I have tomorrow off from working on the ranch—not that they need me. We have plenty of ranch hands, but this is for a good cause. I enjoy helping somebody out. And the money goes to help someone else who needs help with Christmas for their family."

She stared at him, then smiled. "You actually know exactly why they decided to do it. That's nice. I've been hearing a lot of people talking about bidding on you, so you should get a really nice price for the donation, and then you'll make somebody's day. Good luck."

He studied her, then nodded. "Thank you. So I guess I'll see you later."

"I'll be around unless I get called out." She

nodded at him then walked away with her chest tightening up and her stomach rolling. This was ridiculous and that was all there was to it. She needed to get hold of how she was reacting whenever she was around him these days. She definitely planned to make sure that them being around each other remained seldom.

Jake had actually enjoyed the night. Although after talking with Hanna he had made certain they didn't run into each other again. That was just the way it was going to have to be. He visited with people all over the room who he saw often and some who he just got to see every now and then at parties like this one.

Jake saw Natalie step up to the microphone as the band's song ended. Everyone turned toward the platform. He knew what was about to happen.

"It's time for our special event! Is everyone ready to bid on a Christmas decorating helper? We have six lovely cowboys willing to give their time tomorrow to help the woman who wins them tonight. Lew Sander's is going to lead the auction."

Lew had stepped onto the stage and nodded at the introduction.

Natalie smiled at him, then looked at Jake. "So without further delay, I'll call Jake Tanner to come up and we'll get the bids going."

He was first. Jake made sure his shoulders were back and that he was wearing his charming face—at least he hoped it was charming. He walked up the steps. He smiled at Natalie and then turned and smiled at the audience. Everyone was smiling and he spotted his brothers and sisters-in-law all standing together, clearly enjoying watching him about to get auctioned off. And then he was startled as he realized a group of single women moved to the center of the dance floor area in front of him. They were grinning and his stomach knotted, but he kept his smile in place.

The auctioneer grinned at him then at the ladies. "Let's get this bidding started." Lew told the ladies to start the bid where they wanted and remember that this was a donation, and the bidding started.

Hanna stood on the side of the crowd when the auction

started, and to her horror, her chest had been pounding since Jake had walked onto that platform. And her nerves started rolling as she'd watched all the single ladies automatically move to the center of the crowd. They were all smiling hugely.

She happened to be close to the front and could see most of their smiles. She had been talking to a lot of people who had said he was the big draw for the night. And that was why he'd been chosen to be auctioned first. If they could get a big donation on him, then hopefully, they would hopefully get a big donation on the others. Instead of everyone holding out and waiting to bid on Jake.

That actually made sense to her. Therefore, having Jake go first was going to be a winning situation. When the bidding started, she was floored because the bids for Jake started out at seventy-five dollars and then went immediately to a hundred dollars. And continued inching up, quickly reaching two hundred dollars. Which wasn't horrible because this was the year-end deal and people liked giving to those in need, and they also needed income tax deductions. But this was a group of single women in a small town and she had a bad feeling that the bidding was about to reach its end. The next bid went up to two hundred and twenty-five dollars. Suddenly she stepped forward and raised her hand to make the bid.

Instantly the five women who had been bidding turned and glared at her. She cringed, not exactly sure what in the world she was doing. She raised her shoulders and shrugged. When she looked up, she met Jake's startled gaze.

The auctioneer called out her bid and then he upped the bid, and someone instantly met that bid. When he took it up higher again Hanna took it and did it again three more times as the other women bid after her. Finally, everyone had dropped out but three women, and now two of them stopped bidding. The woman still bidding looked strained and this was a good sign to Hanna. One good thing about being a vet, she had money to donate. When he asked for a bid of two-hundred and sixty dollars, she raised her hand and called out, "I bid three hundred dollars."

The woman frowned and kept silent.

Hanna won Jake.

Immediately she wondered what in the world had just happened to her.

CHAPTER FIVE

Hanna had bought him.

Jake was stunned to say the least as he met her embarrassed gaze in the crowd, looking as if she hadn't actually meant to win him. If he had been asked who would not buy him, she would have topped the list. So why had she?

This was really strange, but he realized that he wasn't sad about the outcome. He would get some entertainment helping her, knowing how much she didn't care for him, and yet for some weird reason he'd like to figure out, she'd overbid everyone. Tomorrow could be a little bit fun. Did that make him weird? Maybe but oh well, you had to look at things from a different point of view sometimes.

They called her up to the stage and she moved forward and stepped up to shake his hand. "I think we'll work well together." She gave a forced smile, very obviously forced.

He grinned, then laughed. "Yes, indeed we will." She acted as if she hadn't meant to buy him. That was confusing.

It was time for the next cowboy to get auctioned so they moved off the stage so the auction could continue but he felt eyes following them. He wondered if she knew how much gossip she had probably just started. He knew he was going to get questions like never before.

"What do you have for me to do?" he asked. She was moving fast, as if she was leaving so he decided he better ask for details.

She halted and turned toward him. "Um, well, I've been so overworked that I have nothing done, no lights on the house, no tree up. I have nothing. So when they asked me to come bid—"

"They *asked* you to bid?" This was a total surprise.

"Yes, they wanted to make sure they had plenty of people bidding. So I told them I would."

So that was what happened. "I was wondering why you bid on me. It was a surprising moment when I heard your voice."

"It just happened. But anyway, just come when you want to and you can put the lights up on the outside of the house. I'll have them all ready and I'm off tomorrow, unless there's some major emergency, so I should be there to help. If I had a tree, I'd start putting it up but I'll have to put that off. At least the outside will be decorated because if I hadn't done this, I probably would have just gone through Christmas without any decorations."

"I go through Christmas without any decorations, you know my family all has decorations up and that's where I'll be at Christmas. My thought is why put a tree up at my house when it will just be seen when I go home to go to sleep."

"That's kind of the way I need to think. I'm barely there with regular hours and then emergencies at night. When I am there, I'm sleeping. I guess I'm going to have to hire an aid or a second veterinarian to split time with. I probably won't make it next year by myself. To be honest, as hard as it is on all of y'all with all your animals, it's a blessing to have all this business. My business is growing faster than I expected."

"There's a lot of animals around here."

"Yes, I've found that out this year. Like I said, you just show up when you want to. I get up early and I'll get some coffee made for us."

"Sounds good. I'll probably be there by eight o'clock."

"If that works for you, it works for me."

He chuckled. "Really, how is six o'clock then? Then I have plenty of time to drink my coffee before I start."

She chuckled and her eyes lit up, causing his chest to tighten.

"Eight is fine," she said, still smiling as she turned and walked away.

Jake watched her go and to his surprise, she went in the storeroom and got her coat and then headed out the door. She wasn't staying for the rest of the party. Had he had something to do with that?

She was avoiding all the questions she knew would be coming if she stayed here. Leaving wasn't a bad idea. Except if he left at the same moment, people would notice they'd disappeared at the same time and that would not help the talk that was probably going to happen. He wondered if she even knew the talk that was going to happen.

After arriving home, Hanna stared up at the moon from her back deck. She was just crazy. Why had she bid on him of all people? The moon seemed to shudder as she stared at it, she shuddered too, thinking about what she'd done.

Jake had a way about him that could just seemingly reach inside of her and twist her up and mix her up. She just couldn't figure it out. When they had gone out those two times, the first time she didn't know how she would react, and then the second time he asked her out, there was a part of her hoping that she had been mistaken that they weren't going to be so wrong for each other. She had given him another chance. And it had been a total disaster.

They had gone to a fair and he had held her hand and he'd told jokes most of the evening. He had been funny and made her relax and smile with his humor. Yet, he had also seemed very laid back and uninterested in anything serious. It seemed he was sending the message that he was only interested in casual dating.

When he had taken her home that night and leaned in to kiss her, she'd stepped back to avoid his kiss, despite part of her wanting to experience it very much. He'd asked her if she wanted to go out again, and she'd told him she only dated looking for a serious relationship, and though she'd had a fun night, it was easy to see that he dated for fun. He'd looked a bit shocked as she said goodnight, then turned quickly and gone inside.

She'd been emotionally mixed up because she was strongly attracted to him, but she was not interested in casual dating. Inside, she'd given herself a firm talk about how little she cared for casual dating. She was only dating men who she was attracted to with the potential to become her husband. Obviously, it wasn't him since he wasn't interested in becoming a husband.

After that night, she purposefully avoided him, and she sometimes had a feeling he deliberately avoided her, too.

He never called again, never asked her out again, and she'd been relieved because that prevented her from telling him she wasn't going out with him again. They'd avoided each for the rest of the year, except for the few times she was tending to an emergency at his ranch. But really, as many times as she had to go out there, she hadn't seen him. It had become apparent to her that he wasn't there probably because he chose not to be.

And now he was coming to decorate her house.

She got ready for bed, then laid down and pulled the covers over her. Sadly, she wasn't sleepy, but she knew if she laid there long enough, eventually she would fall asleep. Even if it was only a couple of hours at least she would have some sleep. She was going to need it.

By the time her alarm clock went off at seven, she was already awake. She'd awaken around six o'clock and instantly needed coffee. But she got dressed first, then raced into the kitchen and put the pot of coffee brewing before Jake arrived. She had put on a sweater knowing it was supposed to be cold today. She'd looked up today's temperature last night to see if it was going to be really cold. One never knew what a temperature would be in Texas. It might be seventy degrees and then be forty degrees the next day.

After she brushed her teeth and hair, she then moisturized her face, adding a little bit of makeup base. It was to help protect her face from the elements of being outside in the cold air. She didn't want to damage her skin—plus it did flatter her a little bit—not that she was worrying about flattering anyone. Nope, not Jake anyway.

Just because they didn't' get along didn't mean she wanted him walking around thinking she didn't look all that great. Frowning, she hurried back to the kitchen and poured herself a cup of coffee and took a sip of the hot, strong brew.

She didn't want Jake. She had stopped dating him, so why had she bid so much money on him? She might be losing her mind; that's all there was to it. She paced the house, looked at her watch, and then realized that out of her stress, she hadn't even gone upstairs and gotten her decorations down. She had ten minutes before he was supposed to arrive. She swigged another swallow of coffee and then raced for the stairs. Hopefully she could get the lights down before he arrived. Hurrying up the stairs, she opened the spare bedroom's door, her heart pounding as she pulled boxes out of the spare closet. Thank goodness she spotted the big box that was the outdoor lights.

She had never put lights on this house and hoped she had enough. She picked the box up and had just reached the stairs when there was a knock on the door. Knowing she wouldn't make it down very quickly, she set the box at the beginning of the stairs then hurried back down them. She grabbed her cup of coffee and took a swig before heading to the door. She opened it and her heart started slamming into her ribs.

This was crazy. She had to get control of her nerves.

Jake had one hand holding a bag of something and he was grinning from beneath his tan hat. And her heart, her crazy heart, was doing summersaults. Goodness gracious, she had lost her mind.

"Good morning, boss. I stopped at the diner on the way out and grabbed some sausage wraps for us. But I didn't get coffee since you said you were making that. So, this food is a tradeoff for a cup of coffee."

She was shaken by his smile, so she backed up, pulling the door open wider. "That sounds great. Come in." Grateful she didn't sound nervous, she closed the door after him.

She led the way to the kitchen, which was open to the living room area. The little house had a combination of the living room and kitchen area. And there was a fireplace across from the couch that helped send an extra bit of warmth through the room if it was turned on. Right now, it wasn't on and she was cold after holding the door open.

He sat the bag on the counter. "Pretty rooms."

She shivered slightly. "Thank you. I'll get your coffee. Do you want cream or sugar or anything in it?"

"I drink it black. Are you cold?"

She glanced over her shoulder at him. "Actually, I am. I'll turn it on in a minute."

He headed toward the fireplace. "I'll get it while you're pouring my coffee. It's the least I can do."

She watched him as he twisted the nob that turned the fireplace gas on, then picked up the matchbox from the mantle and pulled out a match. Within less than a minute the flames rose up. When she had bought this house, she had done it partly because it was a whole lot easier for her to start a gas fireplace than to start a fireplace with no gas or anything. Obviously, he knew how to do it too. She hurried to pour his coffee since she had been watching him. She carried it over to the bar and set it down for him. He slipped onto the barstool and smiled.

His amazing smile.

He took a drink also then set it down and reached for the paper bag. "Pick what you want. They make good breakfast rolls."

"They are really good. I have them in the mornings when needing to eat in between emergency calls or heading to work. Thank you."

"You do work some crazy hours. Sometimes it looks like you need some help. I know that time you came out to help us with that starved horse we took in when the sheriff's office asked us, I think you'd been up a long time working. And I know you've been out at the ranch a few times when you had to stay up most of the night. I don't see how you do it." He took a bite of his sausage breakfast roll and his eyes held hers.

She was thoughtful for a minute, because what he said was true. "When I took this job, I didn't really know how much work to expect, so I didn't hire any help other than my receptionist. I was floored by how busy I was almost instantly. In all honesty, I have been thinking about putting out an ad for another veterinarian to join me. I'm kind of exhausted right now and stay that way most of the time."

"I thought you looked kind of exhausted, but I didn't want to say anything. It's none of my business but you've got a big business going and it seems the right thing to do. Like right now, how are you not working?"

"I have a contract for help in emergencies when I really need a day off. Or when there's a major emergency and I can't leave to help at another emergency. The clinic they come from is in Blanco."

"Well anyway, I think it's time for me to get started on your lights." He stood.

She stood. "Oh, I actually forgot to bring them down last night so that's what I was doing when you knocked on the door. They're sitting at the top of the stairs in a box. I'll go up there and get them."

"No, I'll go get them. You finish your breakfast." He turned and walked across the living room and headed up the stairs.

The man had an amazing physique and she found herself staring. She wanted to slap her cheek and tell herself to quit looking. Instead, she took a bite of her sausage roll and a big swig of coffee, then walked to the front door and pulled it open for him. By the time he had put the box down on the porch table in front of the swing, she had taken another drink of her coffee, needing all the caffeine in it to help her move forward. Then she set the cup on the porch railing and watched him lift the lid off the box.

"I'm not sure how many lights I have in there. My rental property was smaller than this so hopefully we can at least do the front of the house. I'm not sure we'll be able to do along the side, and if not, we'll get what you can do done and I'll be happy for the lights."

He toyed with the lights and looked at her. "Or I can run and buy some, then come back and finish it for you. That's my job, what you paid all of that money for me to do."

"If you're sure, then okay, that's the plan but hopefully there will be more in the box than I suspect."

"I brought my tools also, just in case you didn't have the right things."

"Wow, you're prepared." She walked off the steps in front of the house and turned back with her hands on her hips as she looked at the roof. "Thankfully, it's a little house for a single person and it shouldn't be too hard to do. But it will look good with a little color on it."

He walked down to stand beside her. "I think it's cute and it will look real good with some lights.

Therefore, I'm fixin' to get started. Do you want the lights in the obvious place, strung across the front there and up on the little peak above the porch? Then if we have more, we'll go to the sides or we'll go get more to do the sides. We can get enough to stretch across the roofline too. And I'm sure you have a back porch, if you want me putting them on the back porch we'll get plenty and we can do that too."

She stared at him. "I feel really bad because in all honesty, I assumed you would just do what you had to do, then you would get out of here."

Jake shrugged. "One thing about me is I committed to do this and you paid a lot of money for a charity. So, for me not to come through for you would really say a bad thing about me. Not that I'm worried if someone wants to say something bad about me, but in the long run it makes me feel good about myself for you to like what I've done."

She took a deep breath and let it out slowly. "That's a good way to feel and I'm excited about what you're planning to do. I'm going to go upstairs and pull out some decorations for the living room that I can do while you're working, or can I help you out here? You're going to be on a ladder, do you need me to stand by the ladder and make sure it doesn't fall?"

"Nah, I probably won't fall and speaking of ladder, I brought one if you don't have one."

She closed her eyes and let out a big sigh. "Oh, my goodness, I don't have one. You can tell I have had a long week and my brain is weary and I just didn't think of everything. But thank you." She hurried up the steps and into the house feeling like an idiot. How could she have done that?

Hopefully, if she were lucky, he would just think she had not had enough sleep.

CHAPTER SIX

He was grinning after she walked into the house. She was obviously embarrassed since she was clearly showing how tired she was. She did work too many hours and needed help. When they'd gone on the two dates, they hadn't talked about her business that much but at that time she wasn't as busy as she was now. That was when she had first come to True Love, and the year had passed by quickly and her business had grown just as fast. He knew she would stay busy because there was a huge need for her here.

He went to his truck and unloaded his ladder. He walked to the edge of the house and set it up. Thankfully the ground was fairly sturdy, and he wasn't worried about it being unsteady. He went over and got the lights out and realized that he needed a plug so that he could make sure the lights worked before he put them up. He looked around and found an outlet on the porch and went over and plugged one string of lights into it at a time. He was surprised that each one of them worked. They were colorful lights he saw and thought it would look good. When he arrived here, he'd been uncertain what kind of lights she would have, white lights or colorful lights. He liked that she had colorful lights, his favorite.

He climbed up the ladder and got busy putting the first string of lights up: hammer in the nail, bend it over the string of lights to hold it in place and then he would put up the next section. He could fasten two sections of the string of lights held by two nails, then he had to climb down and move his ladder further down the roof. The fourth time he had climbed down and the ladder was almost to the end of the front of the roof, Hanna came outside.

She walked closer to him as he climbed back up the ladder. "Are you sure I can't help you? I could hand you the lights—" She stopped talking for a second, her face turning serious. "Well, that really won't help you because you have to get off the ladder anyway."

He grinned, having been completely drawn in by her offer and the look on her face. "That's the reality of it. I have to get off the ladder anyway so that's why you don't have to help. But it's your house so if you want to help, you're welcome to."

"No, I'll let you do it. I just looked out the window a few times and felt weird seeing you having to go up and down like that. And well, you're fixing to start on the top part going up the arch there and it's higher and 1 just thought somehow I could help. It looks more dangerous."

"I do have to go up the ladder a little bit further as I climb up there and stretch out from it a bit more. But it's fine."

"You know what?" She walked closer. "I'm a veterinarian and I treat a lot of hurt animals, not that you're an animal, but I will feel better if I hold onto the ladder while you're doing that so you don't get injured."

He shrugged and gave her a little smile. "Then you do that. I mean, I'm here working for you so if you want to be my lifeguard or whatever you want to call it, go for it."

She met his gaze, nodded and looked uncomfortable. This was actually kind of entertaining. They were so odd together. So much more than anything he had ever envisioned. He hammered the nail in around the string of lights, then leaned over to the side slightly and did it again. He'd reached the corner, so he climbed down the ladder, feeling a bit off-centered by the thoughts going through his head as he stepped to the ground beside her.

"I'll move it around the corner then get started on the lights going uphill."

"And I'll hold onto the ladder."

He nodded, then relocated the ladder and made sure he had enough nails in his pocket before he climbed up the first part of the steep roofline. She held onto the sides of the ladder and with the low nine-foot beginning of the roof's edge, her head was even with his hips as he looked down at her. She looked up at him, and he felt like he was a crazy man. He knew this because he realized he could look at her all day long. Something about this woman just drew him to her.

He looked away knowing that that kind of thinking was going to do nothing but cause him problems. "You're doing a good job down there," he said as he worked. "I've felt safer than I felt in a long time." Teasing her? What was he doing?

"Well, if that's the case with me down here, then that's great. Just don't wiggle this tall ladder too much or you might end up at the hospital."

He hammered in a nail and then bent it around the string of lights. "If I fall, then you'll have to finish, so hold on tight if that's not what you want."

His thoughts flew back to their two dates. He had thought that they would be a good connection, both busy and just needing some time out. But something about her questions had him realizing that she wasn't looking for a guy like him. A guy who was at the moment, just out to have a good time. She was just as busy looking for a husband. And that was what his brothers were hoping would happen to him. But he was holding off and he had a feeling she had picked up on that because on that last date, that second date, she had avoided kissing him. Their kiss the first night had been really good, actually the best he'd ever experienced but she avoided it the second date and he realized she didn't want to have a relationship with him.

"Jake, is something wrong?" Hanna asked, bringing him back to the moment.

"Yes. I was just making sure the first section heading up was in the right position. I'm coming down to move the ladder." And with that, without looking at her as he tried to clear his thoughts, he climbed down and reached to move the ladder. His right hand instantly wrapped around hers. Their eyes met and his heart slammed into his ribs. "Sorry." He lifted his hand allowing her to pull hers away.

"It's okay. I didn't move fast enough." She stepped back as he picked the ladder up and moved it over.

He looked around, needing some space from this moment. "We only have one more string of lights. You can't have just the front and one side of the house with lights, so I'll go to town and get some more and get them up."

She swallowed hard. "I think I will go with you. We need to make sure we get the same kind of lights and we want to get lights for the front porch railing. I think it will make everything look really good. Oh, and like you said, lights across the back porch will look nice."

He might be in trouble. His nerves were feeling shot and shaky. "I guess we're ready to go get you all the supplies you need for anything you want me to do."

"I'll go get my purse."

He watched her hurry into the house, his heart racing faster than she was moving. This was definitely an odd day. And he had better be careful.

Why had she come to town with him?

Her insides wobbled as if she were balancing on a rope.

"I'm thinking we can go to the small hardware store in town, and maybe not find what you need, or we can head to Fredericksburg. It's just around twenty to thirty minutes away. It will have what you need."

"You're right. Let's do it if you have time."

"I do."

She was losing her mind. She should have told him he'd done enough, and instead, here she was making the day even longer with this trip. They got in his truck and he headed down the road. Feeling nervous, which really shook her up more, she spent as much time as possible pointing at each country home they saw decorated. Jake made comments but he was fairly silent as he drove. He seemed lost in thought. He was probably wondering why he'd mentioned driving her to Fredericksburg.

"This wonderful Christmas store on Main Street draws tourists all year long, I hear." She glanced at him as he pulled the truck into a parking space as close to it as he could get.

"The whole town draws tourists all year long, but yeah, this Christmas store has a great draw."

She got out of the truck and headed to the store. Jake fell into step beside her and held the door for her when they reached it. When she entered, she spotted the lights and went straight to them. Jake came to stand beside her and she glanced up at him. "Do you want smaller strings of lights or the longest we can find?"

"I think longer is better. The less we have to plug them together will be helpful."

"Okay, whatever you think. There's the right color."

He reached for the lights and pulled about ten boxes off the rack. "I think this will be enough for what we measured. But if you are thinking about doing something else we need to get more."

"No, nothing more. I think that's probably going to work. Now we'll get some shorter ones, though to go around the front porch railing. We don't need the great big lights or long strands." She pulled the boxes off the rack and put them in the basket then she looked around.

"What are you looking for?"

She grinned at him and he smiled back. "I don't know I haven't been in here before. Do you mind if I take a quick look around?"

"I don't mind at all. Enjoy yourself. I have to say I haven't been in a Christmas store in a long time either."

They walked down the aisles looking at different things, a lot of tree decorations that she scanned but passed on quickly because if she got started, they would be there all day. However, when she reached the rugs, she looked at them and decided to pick one out for her front porch to finish out the decorations. "I like the one that says HO, HO, HO Have a Merry Christmas," she said, glancing at Jake.

"I do too."

She picked it up and put it in their buggy. Then she moved on and saw green strings of artificial pine garland. "These would look good with the lights on the porch railing."

"It would look really nice."

His words surprised her because he sounded serious. Not just like a guy saying what she wanted to hear. "Do you decorate your house? I thought you said you didn't."

He chuckled. "Like I said, I've got everybody

else's house to go to for Christmas, so why waste my time decorating my small place?

She was realizing that he wasn't home that much it didn't seem like. "So you're really not at home that much?"

"Not really. I sleep at my little house on the property. It's a small place that was used for workers for years. Then I took it over because I didn't see a reason to build myself a bigger place yet. I decorated it some, you know, made it comfortable for me when I am there. I plan to build a house someday but not ready at the moment. It's a little pathetic, but all of us have plenty of money to do whatever we want to, but I prefer to live in that little house right now—without Christmas decorations."

She almost laughed. "You don't want to put them up or take them down?"

"Bingo. But I have no problem helping someone who needs it. But think about how little I'd see the decorations. Maybe as little as you'll see yours. At least until you hire help to split emergencies with."

She shrugged. "You're right, but I'll leave the

lights on, so when I drive into the driveway after a long day at work, it'll lift my spirit to see the lighting. It's not always about how much you're there, it's about the greeting you get upon arrival."

They headed toward the front and placed the items on the checkout counter. She pulled out her bank card and held it out to the checker as she finished.

Jake picked up the two bags in his arms. "It's eleven o'clock. Since we're in town, do you want to go grab lunch?"

They headed for the door and she pushed it open for them. "That sounds good, but I'll buy it since you are doing all this work for me today."

He laughed. "Sure, if that's what you want to do."

"You're doing a great job for me. Where do you want to eat?"

He opened the truck door and placed the bags in the backseat. "How about across the street. We can eat outside there under an umbrella and listen to the singer who is on the porch."

She had been hearing the man singing. "I'd love it."

CHAPTER SEVEN

They crossed the street, and since they'd arrived early, before the lunch crowd, they were led to a table immediately.

The waiter came and took their drink orders. Jake ordered iced tea and Hanna ordered water with lemon. The waitress left them menus then went to get their drinks. He set his menu on the table without opening it. She had opened hers and was staring at it.

She looked up at him. "You already know what you want?"

"I like their roast beef sandwich."

"I forget you've lived around here your whole life." She looked back down at her menu.

"So what sounds good to you?"

She closed her menu. "I think I'm going to have a piece of that lasagna. That's something I never cook myself and I love it. Of course, who knows, this could have been bought at the grocery store."

He laughed. "Believe me, if it's here, then it's homemade. And yeah, that lasagna is good stuff. I haven't had it in a long time, but I remember. I just kind of get stuck on the roast beef."

When the waitress returned with their drinks, she took their orders and headed to turn it in before the place got full and busier.

Jake took a drink of his unsweet tea and couldn't help going back to her work issues. "You've been busy since we've dated. I mean, from what I can see and from what I hear, you hardly ever slow down."

"I know and I'm kind of getting tired. I made the decision to hire someone. I'm going to put an ad out. Bring somebody in to help out. The only reason I'm off today is because I called in my relief clinic from out of town. My answering service calls their number, and they fill in for me. But I need someone working with me that the clients know and trust. I'm making a great salary with all this overtime, but my sleep is running low on a steady basis and I'm starting to feel tired all the time."

"It will be good when you find someone to help you. Then you'll have some normal time off. I mean, that's a good decision you're making. And that's how you actually build a solid business. In all honesty, you look really tired. And I thought so at the benefit last night too. Sorry but I think you'll enjoy getting a little bit of rest." He didn't know whether he was too open with his thoughts but when she gave him a slight smile, he was relieved. Maybe he hadn't messed up too bad.

By the time they had eaten lunch and then headed to Hanna's house, Jake was in trouble. He was fighting the unwise attraction he felt toward this woman.

Why? he asked himself. She wasn't attracted to him, although sometimes he got a feeling she could be. But even if she was, she wanted nothing to do with him.

Oh, she had confused him a couple of times,

making him uncertain, but he was not going to press their relationship. He was going to shut down being drawn to her once more.

When they reached the house and unloaded the lights, he moved the ladder and got busy. She had gotten quiet.

He was at the top of the ladder at the peak of the roof on the last side of the house. "You are a great vet but what's the most heartbreaking loss you've had?" He looked down at her and saw her expression froze and her eyes mist. He instantly regretted asking the question.

Before he could tell her that he hadn't meant to upset her, she said, "My dad, but you're probably asking about an animal. They don't compare to my dad. He was a great guy and he loved being a vet. And I would go with him sometimes all through my school years. I loved it. It was our time."

Jake hated he'd asked the question but was also interested in finding out about what happened. He put the light strand in the nail hook then climbed down the ladder.

She looked at him. "I was already wanting to follow in his footsteps by the time I graduated and was signed up for college with that in mind. I was still working for him that summer before I moved to College Station for the beginning of college at A & M. I wanted to graduate college and go into business with him. But that day, I hadn't even started college yet. He had to check on a bull that was having problems and I rode out with him. He told me to wait in the truck and he headed over toward the bull. It was a total surprise when the bull suddenly raised its head, stared at my dad and then went crazy. I mean literally crazy as it raced toward him, knocked him down, then spun and began jumping up and down on my dad. It was horrible and I didn't know what to do. I started to get out then instead slid behind the steering wheel of the truck and blasted toward them with the horn blaring. The bull jumped away from Dad, then looked at me and raced off."

He was floored. "I'm so sorry."

She ran her hand through her hair and looked so devastated. "I grabbed my phone and dialed 9-1-1. I told them what had happened and where we were and they sent out an ambulance. I had jumped out of the truck and dropped to the ground beside Dad. He was knocked out, but I could see and feel that he was still breathing, but he looked horrible, so torn up. I lifted his head into my lap and I was crying and begging him to wake up, to hold on, but he was bleeding everywhere. My dad suddenly opened his eyes and in broken words told me he loved me, told me not to let a crazy bull ruin my dreams. Then, he closed his eyes again.

"He was still breathing when the ambulance arrived and loaded him up and I rode with them to the hospital. He died before we arrived, though they tried to resuscitate him. By the time we arrived at the hospital they announced him dead. That is the story of my dad and the worst animal I've ever known. Anyway, so now you know. I started to change my mind about becoming a veterinarian, just thinking about it was hard during that summer while I mourned my dad. But I heard my dad's last words to me and started class when it was time."

Unable to stop and completely startled by her story, he wrapped his arms around her, hugging her close. "You went through a terrible, hard time. I'm really sorry for you." He leaned back and looked at her. "But I'm sure your dad is very proud of you. You are an amazing vet."

She looked through her tears at him. "Thank you. I work really hard to be. I want to want to make my dad really proud, even though he's not alive, he knows what I'm doing."

Her words were touching. "Yes, I'm sure he does. So now, we have to make sure this house is super good looking because I want to make him proud too. I want to make him proud of what I helped his daughter do, his hardworking excellent veterinarian daughter."

"Yes. Now, let's get back to it because I don't want to stand in the middle of my yard having an emotional downfall."

He patted her shoulder realizing that he really didn't want to let her go. But he had to. "Alright here we go. I'm back up the ladder." He let her go and moved the ladder.

She needed these decorations, and he was set to get it done for her.

She wiped her face as he climbed up the ladder. She hadn't meant to let her emotions about her dad this time of year show. Her dad had been the most important person in her life. She was looking for a guy like him to one day marry. She had been completely startled by Jake's reaction to her story. When he had climbed down that ladder and gently taken her into his arms, every cell in inside of her reacted. She had loved it.

Loved it.

Which was a terrible thing because he had a party spirit inside of him and was not husband material. His history proved that he liked to go out and party too much and he liked different women. Why had she bid on him? Why would she want to marry someone who even had a small love of that?

No, she was looking for a strong man who would be dedicated to his family. Her mother had died before she had any memory of her and her dad had been everything to her. He hadn't been a partier but instead had been dedicated to her and the business that supported them.

She was so leery of Jake's past. She honestly tried not to pay much attention to him since that last date, but she knew he never dated long after a friend told her he'd been prominent in the tabloids a couple of years earlier with all his dating. Shocked, she knew that meant he wasn't the type of man who would make a good choice for a husband. He wasn't on the front cover or in the tabloids or inner gossip pages as far as she knew these days and at least that was good. But still, his past was there.

And she'd been drawn to look copies up online to check them out. She had been totally blown away to see him in the magazines more than any of his wealthy brothers. It was because he had dated like crazy back then and gave the tabloids more stories. Could someone who had done that change? She didn't think so and her only goal in dating was looking for a husband to share her life with.

She honestly didn't have that much spare time, so wasting time on men like Jake was not on her list then or now, she told herself. Then why had she bid so much money on him last night in order to win him and get him here today?

She hadn't understood why then or now, but she had a problem, because he did not seem like the crazy party guy that she had labeled him. He seemed like a nice, caring man who liked to do good for people.

"Hey down there, are you awake?"

She looked up at him and he was studying her from beneath his cowboy hat. Her heart jumped. "I'm fine. I just got lost in thought. It really looks good, great. I'm glad I bid on you last night."

He took in her words, hammered the last nail in around the string of lights then climbed down to face her. "I am too. This is fun and I like being helpful to you."

She watched him move the ladder and went to help move the lights that were lying on the ground. He was almost through with the roofline lights. She watched him climb back up the ladder.

"This is almost done, then I'm planning on helping you with your porch. It will look very festive, I think."

She smiled at him. "Great. Would you like a glass of water?"

"That would be great. And believe me, you don't have to hold the ladder when I'm this close to the last portion of the roof. I'll be fine."

"Okay, then, I'll be back in a moment." She meant it too. She wanted to be outside with him as long as he was here.

CHAPTER EIGHT

Jake had pushed his romantic thoughts about Hanna from his brain as he watched her head inside for water. Getting romantic ideas might be the wrong move on his part but she seemed different, maybe even attracted to him. He finished the lights and had just climbed down the ladder for the last time when she returned carrying his glass of water. When their eyes met, he knew he was in trouble.

They hadn't been around each other this much since she'd ended their second date. Since she'd told him they weren't a match and he had lived with it, made himself deal with her declaration. Avoided her and obviously that had been a way to avoid feeling this strong attraction he felt for her.

She looked a little hesitant as she held the glass of water out to him. He reached for the glass and their hands touched—he froze. Fire shot up his fingers, his arm, and straight through his body. He had never had reactions to anybody like he had to her. This had happened the first time he had touched her hand and that had made what had been going on with them even harder. He had put off the thoughts of it after she had walked inside that house and never looked back that last date.

Now he held her gaze, her wide beautiful eyes, and he had to force himself to take the glass. His heart pounded. "Thank you," he said, his voice a bit scratchy.

She nodded and took a step back, looking nervous. "You're welcome. So are we heading for the front porch?"

"Yes, we are." His awareness and attraction for her was going crazy. He needed to back off, get it under control. Take this slow if he thought there was any future between them. The very thought shook him.

He wasn't interested in a serious relationship and

he'd told his brothers that just yesterday. Or this morning, his thoughts were confused, and he couldn't even remember when he had conversations with everybody. But he felt like she was interested in him.

He set the water down on the porch. Being won in the auction by Hanna had been an opportunity he realized. A chance to find out why she had stopped dating him, the real reason, because he'd never felt like she'd told him everything.

When their fingers had touched on the glass of water all he wanted to do was pull her into his arms and kiss her, which was what he wanted right now when their eyes met.

"Ready?" he asked, needing to get busy. "I need you to show me the way you want the porch railing decorated."

She nodded and moved to the railing. "It confuses me how to do the top and the railing holding it up. Do we wrap a little bit around the top then wind it down the railing and back up then continue with all the rest?"

"Yes, that's what I'd do." His heart was thundering as he looked at her. They were standing close.

"Then that works for me. The rest of the house looks awesome."

"Glad you like it. Alright, here we go."

He focused first on wrapping the green, pine garland around the railing's top and then he began on the lights. He took the lights along the garland, then down the first railing and then back up. "It looks good," he said.

"It really does. I'm so excited." She smiled, looking happy once again.

He continued on as his mind kept trying to mess up the day with questions it wanted answers to, and finally, he had to know. "I can't help but ask why, why did you stop going out with me? The real reason?"

Hanna stared at Jake, her heart thundering. Why had she bid so much on him that she'd won him? Her nerves were instantly shot as she looked at him. "We already talked about that."

He cocked his head to the side, his eyes looking completely disbelieving. "You know, I've thought about this and that's not true. I'm pretty sure you had another reason than what you said. I suspected it but I'm fairly sure of it now."

"Why do you want to bring our past up? I only have you out here to put these decorations on the house. Not to answer questions from our past."

"I'm just curious. I think you dropped me because there was something about me that bothered you. Maybe you just didn't like me but today I haven't felt like you didn't like me. And I think you feel the same way. My reactions to you have been like they used to be, extremely volatile. You make my blood pressure go up and my blood warm up. And that's highly unusual for me. You know when I'm looking in your eyes like right now, I have the feeling that you're feeling similar things."

Feeling shaky, she rubbed her forehead. "Why are you bringing this up?"

"Why did you spend so much money on me at the gathering that you won me? You could have done that on somebody else."

She looked down and rubbed her forehead again.

She looked back at him and wanted to flee but that was the wrong move. "Didn't we talk about the fact that you dated so many women? And I wasn't interested in dating just for the heck of it."

So that was it. "You were on the husband hunt?"

She nodded. "And I should have never accepted a date with you. I knew that you were in the tabloids a lot. And I mean that should have pointed me straight away from you. But obviously I didn't listen to my intuition. I said yes and, well, it didn't take long to find out that you weren't interested in a relationship that was headed toward anything other than a fun night. I realized that dating you would be a huge waste of my time. Therefore, I broke it off."

Somehow it all made sense and he should have known it. "You never even asked me if all those stories were true. You just quit going out with me."

"I knew you had dated a lot before you asked me out and I know those magazines are called gossip magazines but what they said about you and your family and all that y'all had inherited and the change that was going through your family and that you were out there living it up, well that was obviously true."

He had been kneeling as he worked on the railing, now he leaned back on his boots and let go of the garland. What should he do? Should he be aggravated that she believed all that gossip about him? She wouldn't be the only one he still hadn't totally lived it all down to. Yeah, he dated but most of the women he dated found out real quick that there had been a lot of lies in those tabloids. He was not as wild as they made him out to be. Now, when he was younger he had been a little more out there but he had never been what those tabloids said he was.

"Well, okay, so all I can tell you is you shouldn't always believe the tabloids even if they got somebody in it as many times as they like to put me in there. Anyway, you act like there's some interest still."

She looked away and he reached out unable to stop himself and put his hand around the side of her face and eased it back to where she was looking at him again. "Why do I feel like you were attracted to me and you stopped because of what you thought? Now I guess I can't believe you can talk to me and not believe me despite your obvious reactions that tell me you feel more than you're admitting to."

She blinked and her eyes dampened and he felt bad, but he couldn't help it. She was the one who bought him. She got him out here. She was the one that completely reopened the feelings that he had had for her when he had asked her out. He deserved honest answers. "So you're not going to even try to answer?"

"I need to go inside. You can finish this on your own. I'm sorry if, like you say, this was completely my wrong assumptions, but I can't take it back. Even if it wasn't true, you dated a lot of women and you still do from what I can tell. I'm looking for someone who is in the same place I am, someone who knows what they want and is steadily looking for them. I'm not looking for someone dating everybody and anybody like you do." With that, she stood up. "And that reminds me that I've made a huge mistake today." She looked highly upset as she stepped back. "Thank you for all you've done today. You're almost finished and are free to leave. Bye, Jake." And then she turned and walked into the house.

Jake stared at the door. This was ridiculous. Why was he even asking her things like that?

He needed to just finish up and get the heck out of there, and that's exactly what he did.

CHAPTER NINE

Hanna hadn't slept much by the time she reported to work Monday morning. Thankfully Saturday and Sunday, as far as business went, had been fairly slow and her stand-in had easily handled it. She, on the other hand, had barely handled what she had been through with the up and down emotions with Jake.

She could not help but think about Jake the past two nights. Saturday, she had forced herself not to go back outside, forced herself not to look out the window, but when she heard his truck start, she had gone to the window and peeked out and watched him leave. Her heart had raced, and her stomach felt as if it needed to empty itself. She had been truthful with him, and yet looking at him while she was telling him all of that had felt so wrong. His expression had at first been a little shocked, but then he had immediately straightened it up. Thinking about it now, he had looked just like he was carefully taking what she said without showing emotion.

The thought back to earlier when he had put his palm on her cheek, and she had wanted to throw her arms around him and kiss him. What was wrong with her? She had asked herself that all night long as emotions fought within her.

She had fallen for him and had to fight it off.

How could she feel that way? She had never felt that way about anyone. She didn't know what falling for someone was like, other than these confusing emotions she was having for Jake. It was just infatuation with him, despite that they weren't meant for each other. And yet, when he talked about how the tabloids had overdone stories about him, she wondered if that was true.

Had they gone overboard?

The question bugged her as she got dressed and headed in to work.

The truth was, she had never given him a chance and she suddenly felt very guilty. But it was clear that he was someone who dated a lot, so why did she feel guilty?

She walked into her office and dropped into her desk chair.Tina, her receptionist, came in with a cup of coffee, which Hanna picked up immediately. "Thank you, I needed this," she said and took a sip.

Tina looked concerned. "I thought when I saw you walking in that you looked like you could use it. Did you have like a hard night?"

She took another sip and let the strong blend of coffee and the heat run down her throat. "I just had a couple rough nights. Anyway, how does the day look? I'm looking at the appointment book and it looks like we have a pretty good day for dogs and cats. I'm actually kind of relieved. Friday was rough when it came to cattle."

"Unless we have an emergency, you have no cattle today. However, you and I both know that usually cattle emergencies happen in the evening. If someone makes an appointment for them, it's not really an emergency."

"True. Anyway I say we've got about fifteen minutes before the first client arrives so would you just take them to a room and give me a few minutes to drink this and look through my email?"

"I'll let you know when I have them in the room." Tina smiled, then closed the door as she left.

Hanna took another sip of the coffee then opened her computer and ran through her emails. It was time to work and rid her mind of all these thoughts about Jake. After she quickly replied to a couple of emails, she stood and walked over to her window to look outside. She closed her eyes and said a prayer for help. This wasn't just about her and Jake, he had distracted her but she needed help here at the office. Maybe it was that she was so overworked that he was suddenly getting to her so much.

When she'd looked at her email, it had been with hope that she would have heard back from the company she had contracted to help find candidates for the job. But she hadn't received an email from them.

Tina knocked on the door then poked her head inside. "It's time."

"Thanks, be right there." Feeling determined, she took a deep breath and then headed out the door. She stopped outside the examination room and pulled the patient folder from the holder on the door. She was thankful to find a very sweet client and her beloved poodle in for an annual checkup to help her poodle stay healthy.

She opened the door and smiled. "Janette, good to see you."

"Hanna, how are you doing? It's been a little while since I was in here because this cute pup hasn't had any problems. But I'm still bringing her in for her annual checkup. I think that's what keeps her healthy. You're very good."

"Thank you. I agree with you. I'm doing good, now let's take a look at this cutie pie. How's Princess doing today?" The cute pup wagged its tail and looked up at her with a wide-open mouth. She chuckled. "She's always smiling, isn't she?"

"Oh yes, she's just a happy pup. And she likes you a lot."

"And I like her a lot."

She started doing a quick checkup and saw Janette watching her. She paused. "Is something bothering you, Janette?"

"No, not bothering me. I'm excited. I passed your house on Saturday and I saw that handsome Jacob Tanner putting lights on your roof. The house is looking great. That cowboy is so handsome and nice. He always talks to me if I see him and if he happens to be getting gas when I pull in to fill my tank, he does it for me. Then he washes my windows. He's a great guy. I can't help wonder if you're dating him?"

Hanna's heart had stopped beating, and she stared at Janette. "Um, no. I'm not dating him. I went to the town party Friday night and you must not have been there. I won his decorating ability in the auction."

"That's right. I heard all about that. I wasn't able to go. Did you feed him? I heard that was part of the deal."

Her heart stopped again. She had not gone through with the end of the auction. Yes, she'd bought him lunch but that was the deal. She had gotten upset and sent him home. She cringed inside. She couldn't stand it for someone to agree to something and then not go through with it.

She'd done exactly that. "No, not yet. He did the house, but dinner was not able to be done, so it will be later."

"I understand that is a huge requirement."

"It's going to get taken care of. You know I always come through on things I commit to."

"I know you do. I think it is wonderful thinking about what could come out of this. You could have dinner for him, and something could grow between you two. Y'all probably have all kinds of things in common."

When Janette and her sweet dog left, Hanna closed the door and put her head against it—she had forgotten about the cooking dinner or lunch. This was not good.

She needed to call Natalie and tell her what had happened and ask her what she should do.

Natalie helped run the show, and Hanna hoped her friend would tell her that she had fulfilled the deal because she had bought him lunch.

CHAPTER TEN

Jake led his saddled horse out of the horse trailer and waited while Cole led his off too. They had driven out to the far section of the ranch and were checking on the area while they checked up on the cattle they had transferred here recently. They had help, but they liked to do what they could themselves when possible. Today he'd wanted a distraction and had volunteered. Cole had joined him, and he had a feeling his brother knew something was wrong.

"This area is really a nice section of the ranch," Cole said as they rode out toward the cattle.

"I think so too. One reason I like coming out here is it's so nice. When I get ready to build my own house one day, it may be in a small section out here."

"Are you thinking about doing that any time soon?"

"I didn't say soon, it will be later. If I ever decide to get married."

"I'm hoping you are getting married one day. So how did it go at Hanna's house after she won you at the auction? The way you're acting has me worried."

Jake took a deep breath. "To be honest, I have no idea why she bid on me and won. She could have gotten any man in there to put her lights up on her house for way less than she paid for me. Anyway, I'm still baffled by why she bid so much on me, but I got her lights up on her house."

"You sound like it didn't go so well. Someone told me they saw you two at lunch together, so it made me think things were going good."

"She needed more lights, so we went to Fredericksburg to get them and stopped to have lunch before we went back to work."

"So, what happened?"

"We were doing okay, but I couldn't help it when we got back and started the last part if decorating the porch, I asked her why she'd stopped dating me? She didn't take it well."

Cole frowned with concern. "She's a really nice person. She just kind of tightens up when you come around. I think she's attracted to you and I don't really understand why she quit going out with you. So that is what's bothering you too?"

"Yeah. I thought I was over it, but then here I was hanging out with her and just in seven hours with her, I was out there, you know, going to Fredericksburg and going to the Christmas store and going to eat. I realized that I was lying to myself when I said I wasn't attracted to her. I think it isn't very smart on my part to be drawn to her like that. But there I am, and I don't really know what to do. I think she is drawn to me but doesn't think I'm what she is looking for."

"What is that?"

"She's looking for a husband, and that's why she doesn't date that much because she wants someone who meets up to what she's hoping for in a husband. She messed up when she agreed to go out with me because she'd heard about what had been in those tabloids. Those stupid tabloids. When we located all that oil on our property and those tabloids zoomed in on us, I made a lot of mistakes. I was excited about that change in life and went a little bit crazy, and they started splashing me on the front of those gossip magazines. And they lied through their teeth. And she believes all of that she read. Anyway, yesterday when we were talking, I thought she started realizing that those stories she had looked up and read about me had been stretched. But then she still pulled back."

They reached the cattle herd and they halted their horses. "Okay, tell me," Cole said. "Have you thought about proving to her that you aren't like you were a few years ago? They would have a hard time stretching a story about you now."

"No. All I could think about after our second date was getting her off my mind. I had asked for the third date and she told me that she wasn't ready to go out with me anymore. And I have been adjusting to that by avoiding her. Until now. And she is the one who ended it and now started it. And then ended it. And I now believe she's in denial. But do I want to try and change her mind?"

"Well, thinking about my sweet Tulip. I'd do whatever it took to win her as my wife because I love her. You might not be in love with Hanna. In that case, then you probably need to back off and let it go. But if you feel like you are in love with her, you should figure out a way to see her even if you're not dating. A way to spend time with her so she can get to know you better. On this gigantic ranch, you can't tell me that somewhere out here we can't find a hurt or needful animal. One that needs a visit by a special veterinarian."

He stared at his brother. "You are one smart fella."

Cole laughed. "I hope it helps. Being in each other's presence could be a good thing. It's almost like you quit the relationship before you really knew if anything was there."

She'd quit the relationship.

Then he'd walked away.

Natalie came by her house after Hanna texted her that she needed to see her. It was just after six that evening when Natalie knocked on the door.

Hanna opened it. "Come on in. Thanks for coming."

"You're welcome. I'm curious about what's going on. Do you have a tall glass of tea?"

"It's sitting right there at the table."

She led the way to the table and they each took a seat. "That bid I did has caused me a bit of a problem."

Natalie leaned forward. "A good problem? I kept thinking him helping you might be a great thing. Even though I was startled that you actually said you'd bid at the auction on someone. I hoped you'd bid on Jake."

"No, not a good problem. I don't even know why I bid on him. I don't want him."

"Why not? Because to me, you two just seem to match. Y'all both have an interest in animals and he is a rancher through and through. He smiles a lot and is very helpful to all. And you just seem to match up, so it's almost as if everybody can see it."

She let out a sigh. "I am overly attracted to him despite everything. I had managed to kind of overcome that and then this happened. Sometimes you can be attracted to somebody who is wrong for you. I'm looking for a husband. I'm looking for a man who will have a family with me and be a good dad. We can have a life together while I'm doing my thing with the clinic and he's doing his thing with a ranch or whatever he wants to do. But I'm not looking for a life with a man who parties."

"It was several years ago that he got caught up in those stupid magazines. He was younger and he had just gotten rich off of all this oil that they struck. I heard that he didn't do half the stuff that those tabloids claimed he did. Give him a chance. Even if he did do what those tabloids claimed it's been a long time and people change. You need to be more open-hearted and get to know him better. I think you're just judging him too quickly."

Why was this making her feel guilty? She rubbed her forehead then took a sip of tea. "So that's why you ask me to bid. In your heart you felt like I needed to try again. You felt like there was something between us?"

Her friend nodded. "I just couldn't help myself. You're looking for the man of your dreams. You're looking for the man to build your life with and as far as I'm concerned, you far too quickly bypassed a guy that could truly be him."

"I called you here because when he came out on Saturday. I know that my part of him coming out here and doing this was the money and then providing dinner for him. Well, by two o'clock, he had all this done but we kind of had a little bit of a disagreement and he left. I had bought him lunch at the café when when we went to get extra lights, but I never fed him here at my house. Do I have to? Or does buying lunch count?"

Natalie stared at her and didn't reply. Hanna couldn't take it. "Why are you looking at me like that? I'm already nervous and upset and you're just staring at me."

"I'm sorry. I kind of got tangled up in disbelief. You have to feed him, cook dinner for him. That's part of it. It doesn't say what kind of meal you feed him. Therefore in this situation, you could fix him a to-go meal and take it to him and leave. But you are supposed to cook it. Or you could do what they actually intended when they came up with this rule and have him here at the house and fix him a meal."

Hanna sighed, this was awful. "That's what I dreaded and that's why I had to ask you. I mean, it's not like I'm going to commit to something and then just not go through with it. I just needed to double-check because, well, he was the one that drove away, not me."

Her friend studied her. "You didn't have anything to do with him deciding to drive away like that?"

Hanna's insides rolled. "Fine, we had a little bit of a disagreement about why we stopped dating. And I realized I had been letting myself get caught up in my feelings rather than my intentions. I know what I want out of a husband and I let my attraction to him lead me off that path. So, I went inside, and he finished the porch and left."

Her friend's expression lit up. "Actually, that all sounds promising. This may have given both of you time to calm down a little bit. You could fix a meal and set up dinner or lunch outside somewhere and figure all this out."

"Maybe so. That means I've got to call him. I'm telling you I should have never agreed to do this."

Natalie stood up. "Well again, I think it might have ended up being the best thing you've done. Now I've got to go because I'm supposed to be at my mom's for supper. As you know, she cooks for me every Monday night as our way of getting to spend a little time together. Good luck. Talk to you later."

After her friend had left Hanna's stomach felt like it was ready to heave and her heart was pounding like it wanted to break free. But she ignored it. She was an adult, she could do this and move on. And that's what she planned to do.

CHAPTER ELEVEN

That night she got called out and didn't get in until two a.m. After so many nights of sporadic sleep, she fell into bed despite the troubled thoughts in her head and she slept.

And dreamed about Jake.

When she woke up the next morning, Hanna knew she was going to cook him a meal and get this over with, but first she had to go to work. And of course, she was swamped at work and then she got called out on an emergency. They had to cancel some of her afternoon appointments and move them to the next day while she went on a call to help a very injured horse survive.

Hanna was worn out by the time she got home a

little after six o'clock. Still, she cleaned up, then headed to the grocery store to get the ingredients needed to cook Jake a meal, then she would call Jake about when he wanted it. The deal was that she didn't have to eat with him. But when she got home and was about to start cooking, her emergency line alerted her that she had an emergency. She was startled to find out that it was the Tanner's ranch that needed her.

Her emotions raged as she had no choice and headed toward her veterinarian truck. She climbed in and started on her way, calling the number the service had given her. Within moments Jake answered—she never knew whose number she'd get from the ranch since it depended on who was reporting it.

"I hear you have an emergency. I'm headed out that way." She fought to sound professional.

"Good, that will be great. The cow is struggling but I think it will be okay, but I need you to assure me by taking a look at it."

Dread curled inside of her like she had never had an emergency situation before. "I'm not expecting to find it dead by the time I get there?"

"No, it's alive."

"Alright, I'll see you in a few minutes. Call me if there's a change." She hung up whether he was ready or not. She drove ten minutes further, then entered the pasture where the directions had told her to come. She drove over a small hill then across a cattle guard and saw a lake with a cabin beside it. What? It was almost dark, but she spotted a shadow of a man standing near the water and she was pretty certain it was Jake.

Instantly her heart started pounding as she pulled in beside his truck and hopped out. Something did not feel right. "The cow is here by the lake?"

"Actually, I need to apologize."

She stared at him. "Are you're telling me there's no real emergency?"

He looked slightly apologetic. "Yes, I'm telling you that. I looked for an emergency tonight but couldn't find one to get you here so that I could apologize to you. So, I made it up. You didn't deserve what I did the other day, Hanna. I got carried away and asked too many questions and pushed you. I messed up."

"And now you pretended there was an emergency to get me out here when I was off," she looked around realizing that the cabin had a BBQ pit at the back, and it was obviously being used. "No injured cow, instead you're cooking your supper. I'm not sure what to make of this except it's me who owes you an apology. I was mean to you, but I had decided to finish my bid on you with the dinner that I owed you. I was actually at home cooking it when I got the call. I planned to drop by your house tomorrow so you could eat it. I guess we are both trying to make up for what I started."

He had his hands on his hips as he looked at her. "Well, I have to say that you wanting to apologize to me gives me a good feeling. I mean, dropping the meal off for me to eat by myself is kind of disappointing, but I understand you're not interested in any personal attachment. However, the way I look at it is we live in the same town and you work with cattle and horses on our ranch often. Since we stopped our brief dating, I purposefully leave if I know you are coming to the ranch, even when I was the one who found the problem. I'm not going to do that anymore if I need you on the ranch. I thought that I could serve you a meal tonight and then we could at least build a working relationship instead of a personal one. I guess I'm saying we could start over now with this meal and you can relax and let this be the one you were planning to fix for me."

"But I'm supposed to cook it."

"You can come inside and help me prepare the potatoes that are probably ready to come out of the oven right now. And then you can take credit for that and let the bid be over. We can at least be working related friends."

She could barely breathe. This was the right thing to do, have at least a working relationship because of all the cattle on the ranch and the horses. But it would, in all honesty, be hard since she was so attracted to him—which she needed to get over and maybe this could help her face it instead of trying to avoid it. "Okay, I will stay, and we will work on a new relationship built around our businesses."

He smiled. "Great, let's do this before you get called out on another emergency."

She followed him to the house, and he opened the back door and waited for her to enter first. She felt kind of shaky. She knew they needed to do this if they were going to live in the same town together. They needed to stop being drawn to running away from each other, and this was the start.

She noticed as she walked into the kitchen that it was a small cabin but nice. "Who lives in this cabin?"

"It's the camping cabin. It's out in the middle of the ranch and, as you can see, it's really small. It was one of the first cabins out here. We updated it and put the BBQ pit in, and we take turns coming out here if we've had a stressful day or we just feel like fishing and relaxing. Then again, we have the barn not too far away if we need it for injured animals this far out. And sometimes all of us brothers just meet out here and we enjoy a meal together. It's a very useful cabin and I thought that it would be a great place for us to start over."

This was so much not what she expected. "It's nice and I think that you had a good idea."

He pulled the baked potatoes in her direction.

"Great. So how do you like your steaks?"

"Medium."

"That's how I take mine too, so I need to get out there and get the steaks off the grill. Thankfully you didn't want it bloody."

"No, I do not. I see enough blood in one day without having to eat it."

He chuckled and headed for the door. She watched him go and then closed her eyes, leaned against the counter and sighed. What a surprise this was.

Jake pulled the steaks off the pit, convinced that this was going to be an unusual but good reason to have dinner with her. Sure, they might not come out of this with anything except being friends, but he was convinced that if he had any vision in his brain that there could be more between them at some point, this would help. He just needed to start with friendship and a working relationship. Then they could know what it was from there.

He walked into the kitchen, set the steaks on the

counter, and then watched her as she was finishing the potatoes. "Good job, hopefully this will be a decent enough meal. I hope you like these two things."

"It will be great. And then you've got this salad here too. We could have just had steak, you know." She laughed as she said it.

"That doesn't seem right, I'm trying to win you over as far as friendship goes, and steak with nothing else probably wouldn't be enough."

"Maybe not." She chuckled, and he appreciated the sound of it.

They carried their plates over to the table he had set up earlier with a pitcher of tea and glasses already waiting. He set his plate down and then quickly reached over and pulled her seat out. "Allow me."

"Thank you. But you didn't have to do that."

"Yes, I did." He sat down and hitched a brow. "But I'm trying to be your friend and business acquaintance, so having dinner with you is a little different for me. When I was trying to date you, that stuff came natural. But we're not doing that today so if I do something you don't care for let me know."

"It was fine. These steaks and potatoes smell delicious."

"Good, just jump in there and get started."

With that they both dug into their steaks and ate for a few minutes. His nerves settled down a little bit and Jake knew he would get used to this non-romantic relationship.

But it might be hard, since the part of him that was still attracted to her was stronger every time he was around her.

CHAPTER TWELVE

By the time she made it home, Hanna was still thinking about what Jake had said about their relationship. It made complete sense and she needed their business, so making their relationship a friendly business one where they could work together needed to happen.

She had things to adjust to—most specifically the attraction to get over. She went into her house, got ready for bed, and dropped into it. Why, she didn't know, as it was only nine-thirty. However, she never knew when she would get called out and not get any rest. So, on nights like tonight she tried to get to sleep earlier. Not that she believed she was going to sleep tonight. Her mind was stuck on Jake.

As it had been for the last few days. She appreciated that they had made it through the night talking about her business. Talking about their businesses. She talked about when she went out on emergencies, and he talked about his enjoyment of being a cattleman and how one day he wanted to raise a bunch of kids to enjoy it too. Jake had added that at the moment he wasn't thinking about kids. He'd told her that his brothers on the other hand were definitely thinking about becoming daddies.

He was thoroughly happy about becoming an uncle, just not a husband or a daddy. Yes, one day he would but right now he was thinking about the ranch. Hanna had been startled by his answer and knew that he might care for her but was trying really hard to adjust their relationship to satisfy her. Just like she had suspected.

Or hoped?

Jake walked into the barn and spotted Cole and Levi at the coffee maker. "Morning, fellas." He moved to the counter and grabbed the coffee pot and a mug and poured.

"Good morning to you," Cole said.

"Good to see you this morning," Levi said. "You can fill us in on what you were doing last night? Yesterday we were over in the pasture on the far side of the road from where you turn to go to the camping cabin. We had taken a trailer out there and unloaded our horses like we always do since that area is so far out, and we were checking the herd over. We had just come over the hill when we saw you turn into the road leading to the cabin. There aren't any cows on that piece of land or the barn right now, so we assumed you were going there to relax. Thirty minutes later we had gone down the pasture a little bit and turned around, and lo and behold, we saw Hanna heading down that road. Did you have a date with her at the cabin?"

"We are very interested," Cole said, grinning.

He stared at Cole then back at Levi. "Didn't Cole tell you about our conversation? We talked and I decided that she and I need to at least become friends. We need to at least be able to work around each other for the business' sake. I think she's really awesome, but she has a problem with me. She basically has labeled me with who the tabloids said I was, not that she was around here then, but she's heard about them and looked some up. When I asked her out she went out with me twice but then decided I wasn't the kind of man she wanted to date."

"Because of gossip in the magazines?" Levi asked. "I never realized that. So that's why if we need her at the ranch you are hardly ever around."

"Yes. I tried to hide what happened and didn't want to be around her. I was shocked when she bid and won me at the Christmas party, and while I was over there working for her, I got to thinking she might be interested again. So I'm not wanting to run her off by asking her out, but I faked an emergency last night at the cabin. I fixed steak and potatoes and talked her into eating with me and discussing building a working relationship. It worked."

His brothers stared at him. Even Cole, who he hadn't told his plan after they'd talked.

"Great." Cole grinned. "Great idea. Y'all need to

be at least able to work on the cattle together. You need to at least be able to work with each other because we all know how many times this year alone we needed the vet. And you left us in charge most of the time even if you were the one who found it."

"True," Levi agreed.

"I didn't stay around when she arrived because it was just so awkward. Anyway, after dinner we came to an understanding about our working situation. I think we'll be able to at least agree to be friends and work together when she is taking care of our animals."

"And what about these feelings you have for her," Cole said then looked at Levi. "He does have feelings for her."

"I can tell," Levi said.

This was a little frustrating looking at his brothers. "If anything is to come out of this it will happen slowly. I think she's awesome and I have never been as attracted to someone as I am to her. But I'm not completely sure about how she feels, though I feel like she's hiding from what she feels."

I believe she's attracted to you too." Levi grinned.

"But for some reason she doesn't want to be. So maybe this plan you have will work."

"I agree." Cole lifted his cup of coffee. "Here's hoping this all works out."

He looked at his brothers. "I'm hoping but also planning not to go too fast and mess up any chance I have with aggressiveness."

"Good," Cole agreed.

Levi grinned. "It sounds like you have a good plan."

"Thanks. But now I have to go check on the crew and make sure they're doing well with the cattle labeling and all that good stuff."

Cole handed him a paper. "Here's the list of them. If it's wrong alert us."

"Thanks for printing this out for me. I'm out of here."

When they called goodbye out to him as he left the barn, Jake heard the expectation in their voices. They were expecting him to either fail or win where Hanna was concerned. And the truth was that he honestly had no idea what the results with her were going to be either.

CHAPTER THIRTEEN

The Saturday before Christmas they had their town Christmas festival scheduled. It was a little close to Christmas this year, but they still expected whoever could would come. Hanna knew the kids from their small school were very happy about that and looked forward to it.

She gathered her coat, because it was a lot colder this week then it had been last week, and as strange as it seemed they were possibly going to get snow.

Snow in this area of Texas was not common but it did happen some years. Last week hadn't been bad but this week was really cold. Who knew what was coming? When she got into town, she parked in a parking area away from where the parade would be.

She walked down the sidewalk to Main Street. Looking down the street, she thought how this was a really cute town at Christmas.

The stores were decorated in unison and she loved it. Further down the road on one of the side streets was where they were having the celebration. It was about an acre and everybody had set up their booths, and it looked like it was going to be fun. A lot of her clients had told her how fun the festival would be, but first most everybody would be lined up along Main Street for the parade. And that was exactly how it looked.

She settled in to watch just as the parade began. It was a small town but cute and enjoyable. She watched trucks with kids from baseball teams in the back throwing candy drive by and kids driving all kinds of outdoor four-wheelers. There were cheerleaders and then the football players followed along. Clowns wound in and out of the group. A truck pulled a trailer full of girls, young to teenaged, throwing candy. All the kids along the street were rampant about picking up the candy. She smiled, loving it all. And then she saw the cowboys she had been waiting on riding in the parade. Her heart sped up the moment she spotted the Tanner men riding on their horses and leading a lot of other ranchers.

But it was Jake Tanner who instantly caught her interest like he did the first time she'd ever seen him.

When she moved to town it had been right before Christmas and she'd come to the parade. She'd glimpsed Jake for the first time and had immediately felt weak knees fighting to hold her upright as their gazes had connected. And it had been an attraction like that which had made her excited to go out with him. And made it hard to stop dating him.

Thankfully being so busy at work had helped her push thoughts of him into hiding. But now, since the Christmas party, she couldn't stop thinking about him.

She reminded herself their relationship was for business and nothing more. Her daddy had always told her to make the best of all situations, and she was trying to.

Smiling, he tossed handfuls of candy her direction and the kids dove for them. Her stomach rioted as their eyes held. Her insides were a mess when he winked at her and then threw another handful of candy her way, as he rode on down the road with the cowboys. She stood still as all the kids stayed busy grabbing up tootsie rolls around her, and she watched him ride away.

By the time the parade was over, her nerves were calm and she headed to the Christmas festival. Thank goodness it was now busy with all the people who had rushed there after seeing the parade. She said hello to a lot of people she knew and then saw Natalie rushing toward her.

She smiled. "Hi, Natalie."

"Hi," Natalie said, breathing slightly hard from rushing. "Alright, so how's it going since you decided to have dinner with him?"

"Fine. But to be honest, it wasn't my dinner that we had. It was his." She told her about the emergency call that got her out to his cabin. "He had dinner cooked and asked me to the cabin so we could talk about the fact that we needed to be able to work together when needed. He apologized for lying to get me out there, but I understand what he was doing. We did need to start over so we would at least be comfortable in our town. Anyway, that's what we've agreed to. It's not about dating and doesn't need to be." She sighed thinking about the look on his face when he spotted her and then threw her the candy and winked at her.

Natalie hiked a brow. "I saw him toss candy at you and saw your expression get very interesting as you watched him. I'm convinced that you two are trying to talk each other out of something very important between you. But I'm glad you're at least going to be friends. Who knows what will come out of a friendship. Whatever it is, I hope it comes quickly."

Jake didn't normally stay for the festival. He just came to be a part of his family riding in the parade. But after he had spotted his new *friend,* he emphasized the word to remind himself to keep it that way and not run her off. He'd decided to at least say hello. They were on talking terms now, so he headed into the festival.

He spoke to several people when he saw them but

kept moving. He was walking past the hot cocoa stand when he spotted Hanna walking toward him. He stopped walking and waved at her. She looked slightly startled to see him then smiled and came his way. Again, he wondered if she was fighting what she felt for him, like he fought against what he felt for her.

"Hey, how are you?" he asked.

"I'm not having to go out for an emergency call, so I came in to see the parade and all of this. You know, support my town and all the people who support me."

"I totally get it, it's kind of like what me and my brothers are doing by participating in the parade. They ask us, so we do it to show our support. It's always fun and I like throwing candy out to everyone. Sorry you didn't get any of your candy."

She smiled. "I wondered if you noticed I didn't get any of it, but I don't need any. And I enjoyed watching the kids scramble after it."

"That's good. Would you want to grab a cup of hot cocoa? My treat."

She looked over at the stand, then smiled at him.

"Sure, I thought about getting it earlier but then I went and talked to some friends."

They both took a couple steps and got in line. "So, have you had a lot of work this week?" he asked, trying to keep this casual.

"It was busy. And oddly though, there weren't too many afterhours emergency calls."

He chuckled and got to the counter, ordered the two cups of cocoa and then looked at her. "Thankfully it was a quiet week for emergency calls. Real ones anyway." He smiled, and she laughed, which was a relief. "I will warn you, realistically that we do have a bunch of pregnant cows so hopefully none of them will end up needing you tonight. But I can assure you from here on out, if you get a call from me it will be the real thing. I won't be setting you up again."

He paid for their cocoa, picked them up, and handed her one of them as they walked away from the line.

"I believe you. I mean honestly what would you have to prove from doing that again? If you did it, I'd probably never trust you anymore."

"And that's what I thought. You can trust me."

"Great, I will. Now, this is a nice celebration the town is holding." She took a sip of her cocoa.

"Yes, it's a small town but look at this huge amount of people who are here. Texas has many communities and a lot of people just really enjoy celebrating Christmas. And a lot of people come from surrounding areas too. It's a fun time. To be honest though, I don't normally come to the carnival, just the parade. But I saw you and I thought since we started our friendship, I would just come say hi to you."

She stared at him and his gut twisted. Had he messed up?

"Hello," she said with a smile, her eyes twinkling. "I'm here to say hi to clients and a few friends. My friend Natalie and I just visited and now I'm wandering around."

"You've been here a little over a year and you've made friends, right?"

She bit her lip as she was probably trying to decide if she was going to open up to him or anything. But he was really curious. "The truth is that no, I haven't made a lot of friends, but I've made a lot of associations with the owners of the animals I take care of. As far as friends to hang out with no, I haven't made many. There's Natalie, but she's very busy with all the stuff she has going on. You know her mother was really ill this year but is doing a lot better these days. She actually fixed supper for Natalie the other day, which hadn't happened in a while. Natalie was on her way tonight to check on her. So we were glad to run into each other for a few minutes."

"So basically, your being here is for business."

"Kind of, but I'm very busy and tied up with my business, so really getting to know people takes time. But working alone, I do a lot of emergency calls after hours and don't get to hang out at gatherings like this often."

"So what do you do for Christmas Eve and Christmas Day?"

"I was fairly new last year and was going to spend it alone, but Natalie invited me out to spend it with her family. I got called out on an emergency though and spent much of the night helping a very sick cow."

"How about hiring someone to fill in for you?"

"Not at Christmas, I only use a fill-in when I am just worn out. I don't feel right about someone missing their Christmas because of filling in for me so I always work Christmas. Have since before I arrived here."

"You are a very nice woman. I can see you doing that. But you need somebody you can take turns with on emergency nights."

"Yes, I do. And I'm looking already. But right now, I'm here to enjoy this carnival." She knew he was right, but she was here to enjoy herself tonight.

"Then let's walk so you can participate." He started forward.

"Perfect," she said and fell into step with him. Her mind whirled as she thought about him. He just didn't seem like the person she'd thought he was from all the magazine articles she'd read. She hadn't been giving him the chance to prove he was different. But in this friendship situation they were in she could do that without him realizing it. Couldn't she?

A Ferris wheel came into view. "I love Ferris wheels. Would you want to go on a ride with me?"

He looked at the Ferris wheel and then back at her. "You really do like Ferris wheels?" She nodded and smiled. He smiled too. "That kind of surprises me, but I like them too. Let's ride."

They walked over to it and her heart pounded because she was going on a Ferris wheel ride with Jake. They got in the seat and were locked in by the man running it. It was a small seat, so their shoulders touched, and their thighs touched. Heat raced through her like lightning.

He glanced at her and then looked straight ahead. "This was a good idea you had. I would have been home sitting on the porch watching the news or something if I hadn't come to find you."

She looked at him as the machine started moving. "I have to admit that this is much more fun than watching the news would have been."

"I agree." He smiled at her.

The Ferris wheel went slow, stopping each time they loaded somebody else into it. When they reached the top and were sitting there overlooking everything, Hanna's heart, her crazy heart, was pounding unbelievably.

She looked at him. "This is not a huge Ferris wheel but it's going to be fun. Thank you for riding with me."

"I'm glad to be here. What are you doing for Christmas?"

They started moving slowly again. "I'll be at home waiting on an emergency call. It's been quieter than usual this week, which makes me leery. I mean, I know there are several cattle ready to calve, including at your ranch. There could be an emergency from that group of cattle so I'm just hanging around the house on call."

"Since you're not going anywhere for Christmas, you are more than welcome to come to our Christmas dinner with us, it'll be on Christmas Eve. Goodness, you do so much work for us it would be our way of showing our gratefulness for you. I mean, you're more than welcome and I can tell you all of my family would not want you spending Christmas alone."

It was so tempting. "That's such a sweet invitation—" The Ferris wheel jerked as it started going on its actual mission with a little more power than it had had picking up riders. She and Jake both jerked forward. He threw his arm around her shoulders and held onto her.

"Are you okay?" he asked. "That was startling."

Hanna met his gaze and nodded. "Thank you for grabbing me."

"I'm glad I was sitting here." He squeezed her shoulder.

"Me too." She realized she was enjoying the feel of his strong arm wrapped around her as his fingers tightened on her shoulder. She told herself to get a grip.

CHAPTER FOURTEEN

er phone rang as they unloaded from the Ferris wheel ride. She pulled it from her pocket and looked at it then looked at Jake. "I have to take this call from my emergency call service."

He nodded as she answered the phone. When she hung up, she met his gaze. "I've got a bad situation out at the Harris ranch and have to go."

"I'll walk with you to your truck. They have a lot of cattle."

"Yes, they do." She walked fast and they reached the truck quickly.

He opened her door for her. "What would you say if I wanted to come with you? "

She stared at him. "There's no need for it."

"You don't know that, and you have nobody to go with you so let me ride out with you tonight." He hitched a brow. "Come on, let me come along."

She sighed. "Okay fine, thank you."

"This way if something were to go wrong, I'll be there instead of feeling guilty tomorrow when I heard about you being in the hospital."

"I'm not sure whether to be insulted or touched by your statement." And she didn't. Was he insulting her or telling her he cared?

CHAPTER FIFTEEN

It was one of a rancher's cows having problems and he had put it in a stall in the barn. It had on a halter and was tied to the railing.

"Its hind leg is cut and swollen," Bart, the owner, said.

"Yes, she's going to need some medicine and stitches." She got down on her knees and set her medical bag beside her.

Jake immediately moved to stand beside the cow with his hand on the cow's stomach. "I'll be here in case she decides to try and kick you."

"Thanks, but so far so good." She quickly prepared the syringe and then gave the pain shot that would relax it as she worked. She cleaned the injury and put a layer of medicine ointment over it before wrapping it in gauze. She rose to standing and looked up at the rancher. "I think it's going to be okay but keep me informed and if you can't clean it and put another wrap on it tomorrow, call me and I'll come out and do it. I'll leave you a roll of gauze and ointment. I'm giving it an antibiotic shot now." She reached into her bag and pulled out a syringe and filled it with the medicine. She injected it quickly as Jake rubbed the cow's back, to distract it from the shot, she assumed.

The guy nodded. "Thanks. You did a great job as always. We are highly grateful to have you in our community."

"And I'm glad to be here. Call me if you need me, Bart. And Merry Christmas."

When they got back in the truck, Jake could tell she was tired. "It was easy to tell Bart is a fan. You have a great reputation around here."

She kept her eyes on the road. "Thank goodness. I'm working hard, you know, building a new business takes a lot of hard work and dedication."

"And you definitely know how to do that."

She glanced at him. "I got to thinking about it for some reason while we were in there." She cut her gaze back to the road, her heart beating faster. "I'm not sure why I even thought dating you back then was a good idea. I came here to this town to build a business and later on settle down. Not to date looking for a husband immediately. I quickly realized after dating you and a couple of others that this is not a time for me to even be thinking about that. I just needed to be building my business."

"You need some time off to get some rest."

"I realized us deciding to be friends, business friends, helped me get my head clear. I'm building a business which means building relationships with cattle owners like you and Bart back there. That's what I should be thinking about not finding a husband, maybe after I've been here another year. And when I have someone working for me, relieving me some. But I was rushing my personal life by trying to find my future husband. I owe you an apology for judging you like I did. I shouldn't have started dating in the first place while I had a business to build."

They pulled into town and he was glad for this conversation she'd started. "I understand what you're saying. And I'm not judging you in any way because you know now that I'm building my *business* relationship with you. So relax, we're doing good. We're both refocused, and personally, I like what's happening between us. I like getting to know you better and I like helping you. I have enjoyed my evening and I hope that you don't give up on us being friends."

She pulled into the space beside his truck. "I think I can handle that now. Tonight helped."

"Good. Alright, you be careful going home. And honestly think about coming to our Christmas Eve dinner at Cole and Tulip's place. You'd be very welcome."

"I'll think about it. See you later."

He stood there and watched her back out and head down the street, her home not being all that far away. He had a feeling he could be in trouble. Because he was far more interested in her now than he had been before.

Jake had asked her to have Christmas dinner with him and his family.

This was a difficult situation and she thought about it all the way home. She drove into the driveway, turned the truck off and sat there for the longest time just thinking about it. She had been so drawn to him tonight and she wanted to go to the dinner.

He had been nothing but nice since they had met the very first time. And she had judged him on the gossip magazine articles. She felt like a terrible person.

Angry at herself, she went in the house and promised herself as she got in bed that she wouldn't think about anything to do with him in the gossip magazines.

CHAPTER SIXTEEN

The following night Hanna didn't have anything in her way when she got off, at least not at the moment, so she was going to the fire station to help wrap presents.

After going home and taking a quick shower to get rid of the animals' scents, she threw on clean clothes and grabbed a quick bite to eat and headed out to the fire department. Excitement filled her because tonight was the night they wrapped all the Christmas presents that were donated for those in need of gifts in the surrounding area. Last year she hadn't gotten to help because of emergency calls at her newly opened clinic. So, she was thrilled to be here this year and hoped she didn't get called out tonight.

She was slightly early, but the overhead doors of the fire department were up, and the two fire trucks were parked out front. This gave them freedom if they had an emergency and it also left the inside open for the wrapping tables. She saw Natalie and headed toward her. She said hello to people she knew at another table and waved at Jake's brothers and their wives, who were over talking to several firemen.

"Glad you made it." Natalie hugged her. She was the town mayor, so she was in charge of this event.

"I'm glad I made it too. I was so disappointed last year, although I was glad to save a cow. I just missed helping with my first Christmas giving event in my new town."

"I hated that for you but so glad you are here now. There is a lot of wrapping to do as you can tell from the big stack of gifts over there. We have a list of kids and you'll get a list, pick out from the stack what is on it and wrap them and tag them. Then put them in a pretty colored box and they'll be ready to be delivered to the person on the list."

"Sounds easy enough for me. Do I go get started now?"

"You can. There's usually about four gifts per name you'll see."

"Okay, I'll get started, need to in case I get called out."

"Thanks," Natalie said. "But remember there is going to be a good-sized crowd so do a little visiting too."

"I will." She started walking toward the table where the gift lists were stacked.

"Glad you made it," the fireman said as he handed her the list then wrote her name beside the kids' name on his long list. "This way we can keep up with who has what and that they're all done. After they are wrapped put them in one of the boxes that is against the wall. Write the kid's name on the tag and we'll come by and pick it up."

She smiled and then took the list around and found her items. She made two trips since one gift was a large doll in a box. Then a really cute backpack, a package of two coloring books with a package of crayons, and a cute blanket. She was able to carry the last three over to the table in one trip and set them down. She looked up just as Jake walked into the building. Their eyes met and her pulse quickened as he smiled at her and started toward her.

Several people called his name and he waved at them but didn't stop making his over to her. "How are you doing?"

"I'm doing good. Glad I got to come here tonight. Last year I was out in the middle of nowhere saving a cow."

"Sorry you missed it but at least you were saving a cow."

"True. I would have hated losing it. How are you after being up with me so late last night?"

He grinned. "I got a bit of sleep and I'm here to help. Although I'm certain my wrapping won't even compare to yours. I help every year despite not being great at wrapping. When me and my brothers were little our father used to bring us. We would have our own table and we would wrap presents. And they were not good." He grinned. "We enjoyed it, though. You're here early but soon there will be some families here to do what we did with Dad."

"I came as soon as it started in case I got called out."

"Good idea. Refreshments will be over there in a minute so if you get hungry believe me there will be plenty of snacks to eat."

"Good to know." She reached for a roll of wrapping paper from the pile supplied for her table.

He watched her roll it out then pick up a pair of scissors. "I better go say hello to everybody and then grab a group of gifts to wrap. Talk to you later."

She watched him walk away and ran over the thoughts she had last night while lying in bed. She'd been trying to think of him as a friend, instead she couldn't stop thinking of him as the cowboy she wanted to date. Exactly like she'd thought of him the first time she met him and accepted a date immediately. Then she'd gotten on the computer after the first date and all the gossip magazine articles had come up on the screen and changed the situation. She'd gone out on the second date she'd already agreed to go on with him. But, despite her attraction to him, she hadn't been able to stop thinking that he was not the kind of man she would marry.

"Hi, can I wrap on this table with you?" asked a lady who was holding some gifts.

Hanna smiled at her, glad for a distraction from her thoughts. "Sure, there is plenty of room."

"Thanks. I'm Judy," she said as she set her gifts on the table.

"I'm Hanna."

"It's nice to meet you." Judy picked up a roll of paper. "You're the vet, right?"

Hanna smiled, a bit startled since she'd never seen the lady before. "Yes, I am. Do you have animals?"

She rolled her paper out and got to wrapping. "I don't have any animals but I heard a couple of men while I was getting my gifts talking about what a good job you do. They looked this direction and so I assumed it was you."

"You were right. I started here just before Christmas last year. So do you have a husband and kids?"

"No, but one day when I find him." Judy smiled and looked around the room. "I'm a teacher and started teaching here at the beginning of the year, so I've only been here a few months. There are a lot of great looking cowboys here. That one who was talking about you is gorgeous. I think his name is Jake?"

She felt a twinge of jealousy. "Oh, Jake said that? He's a really busy guy but very nice." Her gaze lingered on him as he talked to a couple of men. Her heart raced a little more.

"Yes, he is nice, but he's not around the school so I barely know him. I didn't live here last year, but I heard he was usually up here."

Had Judy come here just to be around Jake?

Hanna finished wrapping her first gift and as she reached for a ribbon and kept her eyes from meeting Judy's. She didn't really know what to say but she did know she was jealous.

Jake had been more than delighted to find Hanna here at the event. He hadn't slept much last night as he spent most of the short night thinking about her. Big time thinking about her. He had crossed the line wanting more and having to make himself keep back.

When he walked into the firehouse, he'd seen her immediately and had nearly exploded with excitement. Excitement he had to control. But then he saw her glance up and their gazes met and her expression, to him, appeared to be was one of attraction.

She had said last night that she believed their relationship was important. But she was talking about their working relationship. He had gone over and said hello and talked for a moment then he'd forced himself to walk away and not take up all her time. Now as he gathered up his gifts to wrap, he wanted to go back to her table, but instead he went two tables from her. He made sure he faced her, but he wasn't at her table—where he preferred to be.

"How's it going?" he asked Herb, the older man who was the postman who was standing on the other side of the table wrapping presents.

"Going good. I've been delivering Christmas packages like crazy."

"And now you're here wrapping them."

The older man gave a grin. "I enjoy it. I enjoy

helping with these because I won't be the one delivering them. People in here always do. Is it the same this year?"

Jake chuckled. "You're right. I'll be one of the delivery people on Christmas Eve morning. Then the parents can get them and get them ready for their kids."

"That's great. Good for you."

"So what are you doing over Christmas?"

"I'm heading to my son and his family in the morning to spend Christmas with them. If the weather holds off. It's supposed to get bad but I'm leaving early to try and beat it."

"I think you'll be okay. I'm hoping it doesn't mess up delivering these presents." Jake set his wrapped gift to the side.

"Maybe it won't. If it does try, I think you'll be able to handle it."

"Well thank you, but I believe it won't get that bad."

"You are probably correct." Herb grinned at him. "I'm going to go grab me a coffee and a snack before I do anymore."

"Enjoy," Jake said and looked up to watch Herb walk away but he found Hanna watching him. He smiled but not before she quickly looked away, but he couldn't help thinking she might really be interested.

As he wrapped the presents his brain was just stuck on wanting to be more than friends. Oh yeah, friendship came into it but, the truth was, he had never been attracted to anybody like he was attracted to her. And he needed to figure out a way to get closer to her.

CHAPTER SEVENTEEN

Hanna bit her lip and cut her paper for her next Christmas present. He'd caught her staring at him.

"Lucky you," Judy said. "Jake keeps watching you. He's interested in you. Therefore, I know it would be a losing battle for me."

Shocked by her words, Hanna looked at her. "Why would you say that?"

"Because it's obvious you've got his attention."

A thrill raced through her body. "We're friends."

"That's easy to say, but it looks different like from his perspective. Surely you are interested."

Not knowing what to say, she used an excuse. "I need a drink. I'll be back." She turned away and headed to the table where a variety of drinks sat. She picked up a glass of unsweet tea and took a drink. She moved to the side and pulled her phone out of her pocket, checked it just to make sure nobody had texted her with an emergency. She was very thankful that no calls were listed.

"Anything interesting?" She knew that voice.

Jake grinned at her. "Didn't mean to startle you."

"It's okay. I was just checking my messages just to make sure I hadn't missed anything from my service. Remember I told you this time of year it's usually busy and I have been. I'm delighted to have a night that seems more relaxed. Of course I could wake up in the middle of the night getting called out."

"Yeah, I was thinking about that last night, when I went with you to Bart's, about how much you are probably out on the road at night alone. It was, well, you know, it was a little worrisome."

He was worried about her and just the very idea sent a thrill through her. "Well, I mean, I don't really have anybody that worries about me, but yeah, it could be a dangerous situation. In all honesty, I have protection on me when I'm out there. And therefore I'm pretty sure I can take care of myself." But she sure did like the idea of him thinking about that.

"I was actually on my way outside for a few minutes to take a break, want to come?"

She had wrapped three groups of Christmas presents so far and she was a little tight in the shoulders so a break would be a great excuse to go with him. "Sure, I've been steadily wrapping so it would probably be good to take a break. There's still a huge pile of stuff over there to be wrapped so I'm sure when we come back inside, I'll get to help out some more."

"Yes, you can if you want to. This place is packed so everybody and more new people are still coming in and everybody wants to get a chance to wrap something. I couldn't help but notice you wrap really fast."

She laughed and walked with him outside. "When I was in veterinarian school I worked at a department store on weekends and holidays, and wrapping presents for people was part of my job. So yes, I wrap fairly fast since it was just me. These days I don't really have any presents to wrap so this is kind of a trip back into the past."

"Now I understand."

They had reached outside and he turned onto the soft grass that surrounded the place. She noticed there were several people taking breaks, so she didn't feel so guilty. They had told her she wasn't expected to wrap the whole time. She was just kind of a person who concentrated on what she was doing and didn't always stop.

Jake paused at a tree beside the sidewalk. "Did you have any problems on your trips out today?" "No, I was finally having to help with births of calves whose moms were having problems."

"I'm startled that we haven't had to call you yet. We've got so many cows expecting in this cold weather and a few have had them with no trouble. But it's usually when you've got as many cows as we have not to have one in trouble. We have someone keeping an eye on them at all times just in case. But it's anytime now that several will be born."

"You're probably right. Especially with this super cold weather that's expected soon."

"That's what I think also. Speaking of cold, snow is expected the day I help deliver these gifts on Christmas Eve. About Christmas, have you decided if you want to come to dinner like I keep asking you? I can pick you up so you wouldn't have to worry about driving in the snow if it were to happen."

Her insides churned. "I really haven't decided what I should do. The snow and lower temperature could promote a lot of calf births."

"In that case, bring your work truck so if you do get a call you'll have what you need, including a Christmas meal."

She took a deep breath. "Okay, that will work. If I'm needed then I'll be ready."

"Perfect. I'm glad you're coming to dinner. Everybody else will be glad too."

Hanna held his gaze then she smiled. "I'm also glad I'm coming. But just to warn you, last year I was out on call most of Christmas Eve and Christmas Day."

He frowned. "Let's hope that doesn't happen this year."

She hoped he was right but had a bad feeling he wasn't.

"You and our veterinarian are obviously attracted to each other. You might think you are hiding it, but you're not," Cole said with a grin after Jake had come back inside from talking with Hanna.

"I mean, yeah, but there's been a lot in the way. I'm trying to whittle that down along the friendship way. I can see that she's starting to convince herself that she might be wrong about me and what the tabloids spread. Hanging out with her when possible has helped. She's going to come over to your house for Christmas dinner with us. Last year she was on emergency calls most of Christmas Eve night and then again on Christmas Day. The woman works herself to a weary mess."

"You seem pretty keyed up on overcoming everything. We will make sure that if we have an emergency out at the ranch, you're the one there when she shows up. We've all talked about it and we know we've got a lot of expectant cows that are always having struggles when they give birth. Thank goodness we don't have a whole herd of them, but when one of them needs her, you be ready because you're going to be the one out there helping her."

He stared at his brother. "So y'all have been working on getting this set up."

"Yup, we are ready to see you married off. And we all agree she is perfect."

"I can't deny that, just that thought pleases me."

"Then get ready."

"Alright. I guess it's time to start cleaning up, huh?"

"Yup, it is at that. And then are you delivering on Christmas Eve morning?"

"I am. How about you?"

"I'm planning on it ,and my sweet wife is going to be my partner. We're looking forward to it. Tulip says it's a good way to start Christmas. One day when we have a baby, we won't be doing it so much, so now is the time to do our part. See you later."

"A baby? Am I missing some news?"

"Not yet, but hopefully soon." Cole grinned as he walked away.

Jake watched his brother leave as a wave of jealousy swept through him. Yup, he was ready to settle down. He'd been trying to deny it, but he was and the few dates he had with Hanna, he'd known she was special. Then she'd dropped him and he had decided maybe it wasn't time to think he might have found the one for him. But he knew now that he was in love with Hanna.

He helped pick up tables while the women picked up extra wrapping paper. He watched her and knew that yes, he was in trouble because of his love. She placed wrapping paper in its box and glanced his way. Their gazes met, he smiled then went back to work, hoping something would open up this relationship.

But he was going to try his hardest to stick to his friendship role until she made the first move. Last thing he wanted was to run her off again.

CHAPTER EIGHTEEN

The next day was extremely busy in the office as people brought their small dogs and cats in for the slightest things. They wanted them to be feeling good when their family members came the following few days. She was busy all day and had a couple of calls after work. By the time she got home, she was wiped out and went to bed.

One thing about Christmas and her busy schedule was that she slept when she could. She made it through the next day and then headed into town to help deliver the gifts to the homes. She said a quick prayer that she wouldn't get any emergency calls. She didn't want whoever she was riding with forced to rush back to town to drop her off at her truck. She wanted to give gifts to these kids, even though she wouldn't see them, it was still fun being Santa.

She parked her vehicle so that she could get out easily if she got a call and then she headed into the firehouse. She spotted the fire chief and smiled at him. "Hi, I'm here to help."

"Good morning, I've got you helping Jake. He's backing in now. Head on over there and help him load the boxes into the truck. Here are the addresses of the spots the five families want them dropped off. They are in the country, so we've given everyone addressed that are close, within driving distance of each other. Not only do we need to get these delivered, we also need to get y'all home for Christmas."

"Thank you, that's very thoughtful." She took the paper he handed her and tried not to look shocked or happy. She just took it and smiled at him. "This will be fun." She walked toward Jake, who was getting out of his truck and saw her.

He smiled. "Hanna, good to see you."

Her heart instantly started pounding. "Guess what, I'm your partner. Here's our list. We can go whenever we have them loaded up."

"That sounds like a plan to me." He took the list she held out to him then looked around and found the boxes. "These are our five."

She reached for one of the boxes that didn't look overly heavy. She carried it to the truck and handed it to Jake after he had his inside. Within moments they had all of them loaded.

They climbed into the truck and he looked at the first address. "Here we go. First house is the furthest out, about fifteen miles. Then the next four are on the way back to town."

"That makes sense." Excited, she buckled up. She had secretly hoped he would be her partner on this trip and was so pleased it had come true.

He turned onto the road out and glanced at her. "Did you have a rough week?"

"A little bit, but I got some sleep last night so that was good. I wanted to be ready for this morning. You know, like I said, last year I didn't get to help so I'm so thrilled to be here today."

"I'm glad you're getting to enjoy yourself this

year. My schedule I can shoot around however I want unless one of our animals has an emergency. It's my turn to meet the vet if that happens and since that's you now, you know who you will be meeting this year. We take turns on Christmas each year."

A thrill raced through her at the news. "Well, it's not like we haven't gotten used to each other, you know?"

He smiled. "That's what I'm thinking too. If I have to have an emergency, then you are the one I want."

Hanna's pulse raced as a smile swept across her face. He was the one she wanted no matter what.

Jake liked her delight in helping the kids, in helping animals and right now, her smile at him was about being happy he would help her.

His heart had been beating strongly since he saw her. He'd planned to ask the fire chief to put them together to deliver the toys, but he didn't have to ask. Obviously, the fire chief was no dummy.

They drove up to the first house's drop off spot, to drop off the presents. The house wasn't fancy, but it was a couple who had two children and were working hard to make ends meet. They drove up to the designated place to leave the presents. Midway up the drive the father had left a cattle trailer sitting there waiting on them. Jake parked his truck and got out, and so did Hanna.

"The gifts go in the back of the trailer."

"I'll open it for you," Hanna said and after he had the presents inside, she grinned at him.

His heart rambled some more. "You're enjoying this?"

"I am. This is a smart idea by the parents."

He closed the door and they headed back to the truck. "I think so too."

Moments later they were heading back toward the road.

"Will the other parents put things out for us to leave the packages in? I wasn't thinking about the kids not seeing that we were delivering the gifts."

"Everybody has left a spot for us to drop the

packages off. Hopefully it always works out. If rain had been expected they would have been stuffed in a large plastic bag."

"Good to know. I'm guessing everyone doesn't have a trailer."

"True, but they have something. The small building where the kids would wait on the school bus is a mile and a half away. That's where we're going to leave the next drop off. They're out of school right now so the dad is watching for us. It's at the end of their drive so you can't see it from the house."

"That's a good use of a school bus stop."

"I think so too. They all have ideas that work."

Over the next hour they drove down some long dirt roads for the last four deliveries.

They stopped at one and left the gifts in a hay barn. He sent a text to the dad and he saw her looking curiously at him. He smiled. "I'm sending a text to this dad so he'll know they are here, and he can pick them up."

"That's great. I'm sure that tomorrow some kids are going to be so happy," Hanna said.

"Because people like you came out and helped. Even if you hadn't been able to come out, you donated money to buy gifts. And that's the important part. If we had no money, we'd have no gifts. But I have to tell you it was nice seeing you there." He held her eyes, enjoying seeing them soften.

"Thank you, and it was extra nice being there. It is making this Christmas special. Maybe more special than any I've had since my dad died."

"Then I'm more than happy to be involved in it. We better get this last one delivered and then head back. I'll drop you off to get your truck and then I'll hope you don't get any calls this afternoon and show up at the ranch house about six."

Hanna was so touched and so thrilled she had gotten to come. He dropped her off at her truck and told her he was looking forward to seeing her soon. Then he'd winked as she started to drive away. She smiled and found herself dreaming of more than a wink.

It was Christmas Eve and as she drove down the

road toward her home, she was wishing for a kiss from Jake.

If she were honest with herself, she was starting to believe there could be more between them. And she was excited to have dinner with him and his family.

Thankfully she had no calls and was thrilled to get dressed for the dinner party. She put on a pair of nice jeans, a blue silk top, and a pair of soft suede shoes. But she carried a long-sleeved work shirt, a work coat, and boots to the truck just in case she had an emergency call tonight, she would be ready. She went back inside and grabbed her coat and purse then headed for the truck.

She was excited to actually spend Christmas with someone. Someone and his family. When she arrived at the ranch, she backed into the spot next to the other vehicles so that she could get out quickly if needed.

She went to the door and Jake instantly swung it open. And her heart thundered.

He grinned hugely. "I've been hoping you were going to get to join us. Please come in. The others are happy you're joining us. They're excited to see you, but I told them to wait and I'd bring you in."

He had wanted to greet her first. She smiled. "Thank you so much for inviting me. I'm excited to be here, and I'm grateful not to have an emergency. But I'm prepared."

Jake closed the door after her and led her down the hall. "Believe me, I think that you've worked so hard that you're just getting blessed with a night off here at the Christmas dinner."

They entered the kitchen area where everyone was looking at the doorway. She took them in, Cole and Tulip, Levi and Rita, Bret and Ellie, and Austin, who was still single like Jake. They were all smiling.

"Hello, thanks so much for inviting me."

The women all hugged her and welcomed her. The men gave her quick one arm hugs and welcomes. She almost started crying from their welcome to her.

"As you can tell, we are thrilled you are here," Tulip said.

"I'm delighted to be here. Last year I worked emergencies and even my years before that while getting my veterinarian license, I worked in a store during that time."

"You didn't go home?" Ellie asked.

"No. My dad had passed away a few years earlier and my mom died when I was seven, so I didn't want to go home to an empty house. Working during the holidays became normal for me. Y'all are helping me break a long habit tonight. And I can tell you right now my dad is smiling from up above." And he was and her mother was too.

"We are so thrilled to be able to do that," Rita said. "You've been through a lot. And I'm so glad you came to dinner tonight with us."

"I totally agree," Jake said, his hand on her lower back. She looked at him. "I'm very glad you are here."

She couldn't tear her eyes away from him. She knew he was what made it super special for her to be here.

CHAPTER NINETEEN

They were sitting around the table having a fantastic meal that Jake's sisters-in-law had all cooked. Rita was telling that the her son Toby's grandmother had arrived and the two had stayed home to spend time alone together before he went to sleep and woke up to the gifts Santa would bring him. It was obvious Rita loved her son and her mother. She apologized for them not being here but knew everyone would understand. And they did.

They were a great group and it had been a great evening.

Watching them and listening to them just made her feel good. It also reminded her of how badly she wanted to get married and have children. Her family, small as it was with just her mom and dad, ended far too soon. And starting a new family was completely up to her.

She glanced at Jake, who obviously enjoyed the evening as much as anyone. He met her gaze and his lips tipped up. She smiled back then focused on Ellie as she told of a Christmas when she'd stayed up late hiding behind a recliner waiting to see Santa come down the chimney.

"I was only five, but when I saw my dad carry in the bike that I'd asked Santa for I gasped, shocking my dad, who instantly set the bike down and came to pick me up. Of course, he did some of that Santa fibbing, telling me he was just helping Santa since he was behind on his delivery. He said he had told Santa to leave it on the porch and he'd bring it in, so I needed to go back to bed."

"Did you?" she asked.

"Yes, and I had a great Christmas morning that I will always love. And I'm sure my dad and mom breathed huge sighs of relief."

Everyone laughed and so did Hanna. She'd been a

young adult when her dad had died and hated it. But she'd been a young child when she lost her mom. She'd been alone since her dad's death but tonight she was surrounded. And she loved it.

Jake had loved sitting beside Hanna during dinner. Now, they were getting up from the table to go to the living room for more visiting and celebrating when Jake got a call. He looked at the name and realized it was his ranch hand who was watching over the pregnant cows tonight.

He excused himself and went into the hallway. "Mike, what's going on?"

"We've got one in a bad way. I think you need to call the veterinarian. This cow is struggling, and I don't see her having this baby on her own."

He explained to Jake the situation, how the cow had been struggling terribly and as bad as Jake hated to do it, he had to tell Hanna. After hanging up and feeling lousy, he entered the living room. "I have to tell you I'm the last one who wanted to do this, but we have a pregnant cow in a really bad way. We need you, and I'm really sorry."

Hanna had already stood up. "Don't be sorry, y'all gave me an absolutely wonderful evening. Thank all of you so very much. Now, I need to get my boots and a work shirt out in the truck and change."

"I'm going with you and show you where we need to go," Jake said. "Come on, let's get your stuff and you change in the restroom in the hallway."

She looked at him. "Okay, then let's go save your calf."

"I'll call you guys later with information," Jake said as he led the way down the hall. He grabbed his coat off the coat rack and headed out the door.

This woman was amazing there was no doubt about it. Yesterday, they had moved the pregnant cows closer to the barn, near the cabin. It wasn't in the same pasture but close. He'd suggested it because of the threat of snow.

He turned the truck on to heat up while Hanna went back inside to change her shirt and boots. He hoped it wasn't a terrible situation and didn't sound like it was something she couldn't help.

She came out soon and he was already in the passenger seat of her truck. "I figured you would want to drive your truck."

"Yes, thanks. You just tell me where to go."

"It's near the cabin, that's where we have moved all the pregnant cows."

"Then hang on, here we go."

They arrived soon and since there was no use having a third person there he told Mike, his cowhand, to go on home and get a little sleep before spending Christmas Day with his family. "You'll get home before the threat of snow comes true."

"Are you sure?"

"I'm sure. I came to help Hanna and it's only going to take two of us. She can take care of cows all by her lonesome so go on and thank you."

Hanna looked up. "Thank you for recognizing this cow was having trouble." She focused back on getting things out of her medical bag.

"Thank you both," Mike said and then headed for his truck.

Immediately, Jake knelt beside Hanna. "What can I do?"

"Just help keep her calm as I check out what's going on inside her. I'll insert my arm and with any luck be able to help her give birth that way." She pulled on her long clear glove.

Jake watched her as he rubbed the cow's neck. Within seconds she had her arm inside the cow.. He watched her expression as she concentrated on her work and liked how intent she was in what she was doing.

"Okay, it's going to be hard, but I need to turn the calf and then see if the mom has the energy to get her out."

"You can do it." He smiled at her as she went into complete focus on turning the calf.

It started snowing before the calf was turned and it was colder as the snow fell. "If she gets the baby out, we're going to need to get them to the barn. She probably should have already been moved in case I have to operate. Can you get a trailer here for us?"

"Yes, I'll make a call."

He called Cole and asked him to bring a trailer so

they could move them. The calf was being born when Cole arrived twenty minutes later.

"Great job, Hanna," Cole said, jumping from the truck.

Hanna looked over at them. "Thank you, but she had it on her own and I really need to make sure she's okay."

"Let's get her loaded while she's standing," Jake said as Cole opened the trailer's door.

"This snow is coming down heavier." Jake moved over and gently picked up the calf that was trying to stand. He placed it in the trailer and was glad when the mother followed. He moved out of the trailer and Cole closed the door.

"Great work, guys. Let's get going, take it easy, though." Hanna turned and grabbed her bag and put it in her truck. They loaded up and followed the trailer through the pasture.

When they got to the cattle barn, he picked up the calf and carried it into a stall and Cole made sure the mother followed.

"Thanks, Cole. Now, head on home and we'll take it from here. I should have brought that on our way out here but wasn't fully thinking."

"I understand." Cole chuckled. "Thanks, Hanna. It's a really cold night, I'm glad this didn't turn out more serious and keep you out in the weather longer."

"Thank you for getting to us so quickly," she said, then went to the railing to study the cow and calf.

"Glad to do it. Call if you need anything else."

Jake went over to stand beside Hanna. "You okay?"

She nodded then patted his arm. "I'm so glad it wasn't worse. She was really having trouble and if we hadn't made it out there when we did, I think it would have been a very sad situation for her and her baby."

He gently cupped her face. "I'm glad too. Thanks." He wanted to kiss her and tell her how special she was and how much he cared for her as their gazes locked. But he didn't. It took every bit of strength he had to pull his hand away.

She smiled at him. "I'm glad to help."

Hanna's insides trembled as she spoke to Jake, loving the feeling of his hand cupping her jaw. She'd thought for a moment that he was going to kiss her and was terribly sad now. "I'm going to stay and watch them for a little while to make sure they are okay."

"I'll stay too. Not going to drive off in your vet truck." He smiled at her.

"Oh wow, I'm tired and forgot you rode with me."

"I'm completely happy to be here with you. But how about while mom and baby get to know each other, we drive over to the cabin for a cup of coffee or a glass of ice water. That would help you."

"That sounds great and I can use your restroom."

He smiled gently at her. "Then let's go. We'll come back and check on them and since you're going to be here maybe, we can just drive through the pasture and see if there are any other expectant cows having problems, especially with this snow. I don't want you going home and then get called out here again in this snow."

"That all sounds good. And the snow is pretty, however, these cows aren't used to it."

"Me either," he grinned at her. "I'll drive, if you don't mind."

"Sounds good."

They got into her truck and he headed across the pasture then over the cattle grid and then the short distance to the cabin.

"I'm sorry to tell you, I won't be having dinner here like I did last time you visited. But we have snacks if you want something. I'll make the coffee while you head to the bathroom."

"I'll have me a little water and a cup of coffee too. If I'm going to get some more phone calls, I need both drinks. You might find me more trouble in your pasture too. And I'll be happy to help if you do."

"Thanks, and sorry but I have that same feeling. I hope not but the weather doesn't help us."

"Exactly."

They climbed out of the truck and went inside the cabin and she headed to the restroom immediately. Afterward, she washed her face, not caring if she washed all her makeup off her because she felt filthy. Staring at herself in the mirror, she took several deep breaths, because it was after midnight and she was tired. Still, she couldn't deny that she had not minded spending the evening with Jake. She hoped things between them would get even better.

CHAPTER TWENTY

anna walked back into the cute kitchen feeling cleaner and ready for some coffee. Jake was at the coffee pot when she arrived. He turned and smiled. Her heart fluttered. She had really gone from believing terrible stuff about him to being inspired by being around him. All he had wanted to do was help her all night.

"Feel better?" he asked holding a cup of coffee out for her.

She took it, loving the feel of his fingers as she grazed them. "Much better than behind a tree in the woods, which I was about to have to do. But you came to my rescue."

"I am so glad to be the one who came to your

rescue. Speaking of, if you need cream or sugar it's right there." He pointed at two metal cups with lids.

"Thanks, but I'm good. After working, it's much easier to have a cup of coffee with nothing in it. And when I wake up really sleepy a strong cup of black coffee is better for a boost."

"I agree." He led the way over to the living room where two chairs sat beside each other in front of the fireplace. He had lit it and it was warming the room and very inviting.

"Goodness, I may sit down in one of those chairs and never be able to get out." She sank down in one and sighed. "I may fall asleep. I know my bones and muscles are going limp right now."

He sat down in the other chair. "If you need to go to sleep, please do. Take a quick nap. We can go look at other cattle after you've slept a little bit."

She took a sip of coffee. "Thanks, but I'm going to drink this coffee. But you've been very helpful to me."

"I'm trying to help make your job a little easier tonight."

"You did. And this coffee is at the top of the list.

And you've been helping me. Thank you, that you're willing to stay with me to check the others. I need to apologize to you."

He set his coffee on the small table between the chairs. "For what?"

She took a deep breath and set her coffee on the table also. "I misjudged you. I quit dating you because I thought you weren't interested in anything but dating and having fun. I now know I made a bad choice and that I was wrong. I believed those magazines and I'm now certain that most of what was written wasn't true. You have been nothing but a helpful, kind person to me. Even out here helping me deliver a calf. I want you to know that I have no bad feelings about you anymore. I think you are amazing. And have to tell you that I care about you."

Had she just messed up?

Was she so tired that she was talking when she shouldn't be? Should she have just gone home and got some rest and then got her head on straight?

He smiled and her heart went crazy with happiness.

"Hanna, I have been waiting, hoping and praying that you would start thinking like that. Willing to give us a chance." He stood up and held out a hand to her and she slipped hers into it. He smiled and pulled her from the chair into his arms and then he lowered his lips to hers.

At the feel of his lips on hers, Hanna's world changed. Every cell, every ounce of feeling in her went off the records of emotions. Why had she been avoiding this?

She couldn't believe it. But she also knew she couldn't rush things. They had been in denial and not really even crossed the dating possibility since they had just been out those two times. It had been different these last few weeks and she thoroughly enjoyed the feeling of being in his arms, feeling his lips on hers.

She enjoyed the emotion filling her, and the way that every ounce of her body responded to being in his arms and having his wonderful lips on hers.

She pulled back and sighed, looking into his eyes.

He smiled at her but did not let her go. "Don't tell me you're going to run away from me right after you have me believing you are interested in me?"

"I honestly don't want to mess up our relationship by speeding things along too much."

"I understand what you're saying and I'm not going to rush you but I have to tell you this, I'm not the guy who would take advantage of you. I am the kind of guy who will honor you, cherish you, and want to give you everything you want. I'm not the guy you thought I was and am so glad you see that now. I respect you and absolutely love being around you. Honestly, I'm trying to decide if now's a good time to tell you or if I'm going to mess up by telling you that I love you, Hanna. I have never met anyone who came close to that and I know you're the one for me."

She couldn't breathe. Her knees had gone weak and she knew he had said exactly what she had been wanting to hear. She blinked back the sting of tears cupped his face. "I can't believe I almost missed this. I've been in denial but no more, because I love you too. And I don't care about anything that happened in your past because I know that the way you're looking at me, and holding me, that what you say is what you mean. Same as me."

Jake smiled. "We can rest easy about that."

And then they were kissing again. And she could feel Jake's heart pounding happily with hers.

All the next week Jake had never had so much fun or been so happy. His brothers were thrilled for him and Austin was too, though he still was not ready to be on the wedding market.

He had met Austin in town to have breakfast together. Austin had just come off working all night at the emergency room. Jake had needed some things from the feed store and so they met for breakfast. All of his other brothers knew what he was getting ready to do and were delighted. They all said they had known it was going to happen.

He entered the restaurant and spotted Austin. He walked over and sat down across the table. He could see his brother had already ordered him a coffee and was grateful. "Morning. Thanks for this," he said and picked up the mug and took a drink.

Austin grinned. "Ordered our breakfast too. So,

you are joining the wedding club with the brothers."

He should have known one of the brothers told him already. "I haven't asked her to marry me yet, but I'm in love with her and am planning on it. I would have asked her to marry me the other night. I was so sure about wanting my future built with her, but Christmas Eve had been long and I just didn't feel like it was time. We had to go check on the calf that she had saved and then we drove through the pastures to make sure none of the other cows were in trouble. After that it was really late, or early depending on how you looked at three in the morning. I followed her home and kissed her at her door then sent her inside to get some sleep. I went home and grinned the rest of the night. I didn't ask her the next day because her Christmas Day was busy at other ranches."

The waitress delivered two plates of eggs, bacon, and biscuits.

"Thank you," they both said before she walked away.

Austin focused on Jake. "I'm really thrilled for you. And for all of our brothers. I guess when you meet the right one it doesn't matter what you've been thinking or how your life has been going or what your plans are, you feel it so strongly that it changes everything. At least that's what it looks like to me."

Jake grinned. "You have always been able to see things the right way. And it's true. I don't care what my plans were, I don't even remember what they were. Right now all I can think about is asking Hanna to be my bride. And I got the feeling after the other night that she will agree."

"Great, I'm happy for you." Austin smiled and took a bite of eggs.

Jake had been about to do the same thing when a thought hit him and he lowered his fork. "You know, when we get married that means that what they said about that garter is coming true again. She was the first female I saw after I caught that garter. Same with all of our brothers. So if you come to my wedding or if you go to a wedding before mine and you catch a garter, it's your turn."

Austin set his fork down and looked at him. "Only if I'm willing or ready."

"I can tell you it's a wonderful thing. When I caught it, I had no idea that I was going to run into Hanna. And now, I count that as the greatest moment of my life. So get ready, my brother, your best moments in life could show up next."

CHAPTER TWENTY-ONE

"You're very serious about him," Natalie said as she stared at Hanna with a huge smile. "I knew it. I just knew it."

Hanna grinned. "I know you did, but you know I had to get over a bunch of internal problems, so I'm glad I did. I'm honestly grateful that he found a way to hang around me at a time when I was trying to avoid him. It's been wonderful this week."

"And now are y'all going to go slow?"

They were in her office having lunch together on a slightly slow day. Natalie had brought lunch after Hanna had called and asked her to come spend lunch with her. She honestly hadn't wanted to be out in public talking about her love life, so she had decided this would be a good spot. They were in the clinic and she could talk openly.

"I want him to ask me to marry him. And I have this fear that after I put off our original relationship, he may not want to rush me. Meaning, Jake proposing to me may not happen for a very long time."

Her friend's eyes narrowed. "Then you ask him."

"I've thought about that, but I just don't think it will mean as much to Jake for me to ask him, as for him to ask me."

"Then just enjoy your time together and see what he does and if it goes on too long, just ask him if he's interested in marriage or hint that you're open to it."

"Okay, I'll have patience and I'll do that. I'm just so ready to be his wife. Sometimes I wonder about myself."

Her friend ate her french fries while she laughed. "Believe me, you are a great person and everybody in town whose animals you take care of is rooting for you two to be together."

Cole had invited them to spend New Year's Eve at

their house with their brothers and their wives, and some others. Jake had told his brothers at the morning meeting at the barn that he had a personal date ready for Hanna. Immediately they had all smiled and understood and wished him luck.

Now, as he knocked on Hanna's front door and waited for her to open it, he prayed he wasn't rushing her. That he wasn't making a mistake.

She opened the door and looked beautiful, amazing, and his heart just went berserk pounding. Her long sleeved dress was feminine as it came just above her knees and flowed when she walked. It was red with a hint of white sparkles. She was beautiful.

He swallowed hard. "I'm speechless."

She grinned. "Well in all honesty that's a very nice statement."

"Darlin', you look gorgeous. And I mean amazingly gorgeous."

She stepped up and put her arms around his neck. "I was hoping that's what you'd say when I bought this dress. And when I hired my new veterinarian to begin helping me in the clinic and help with emergencies."

She smiled, her eyes dancing.

He was overjoyed at the news. "Awesome. I'm so glad for you. You are starting your new year off right. I'm glad you found somebody."

"I am too. She's the young woman who has filled in for me most of the time. She's single and she was enjoying working out here. When I put the ad out, she was one of the first ones who applied. I'm thrilled and really excited about having her. But I'm most thrilled about our New Year's Eve date."

He loved her feelings about the date and leaned in and kissed her, pulling her close. Then, he pulled back, staring into her beautiful eyes. "Let's get this party started. You need to have your jacket," he said, not wanting her to forget it.

She stepped back into the house and came back instantly with a cream-colored knee length coat. "Pretty also," he said, taking the coat and slipping it over her arms. It covered up her beautiful dress and hung down to her knees, keeping her warm as they walked to his truck. He opened the door and helped her into the well-heated cab.

The snow that had landed over the holidays had ended but then had started back just that afternoon, and the ground was covered with a soft layer of white. It was a pretty drive down the road to a fancy restaurant that had great food, soft romantic music, and tonight they also had a special New Year's Eve celebration.

They reached the restaurant and were escorted to their table, where champagne was brought for them. He had requested it when he reserved the table and was pleased when she saw the glasses waiting on them and she looked at him with a smile. "It looks like you're jumping into celebrating tonight."

"You are with me, so of course I am. I want to make this a good night for you. We're going to have whatever you want for dinner. We're going to have champagne as you can see, but only if you want some. And we're going to dance if you want to."

She smiled widely as he pulled the chair out and she sat down. "It sounds like a wonderful evening. I'm still having a hard time believing I'm with you."

"Same for me." He didn't know if he'd ever believe how lucky he was to have her in his life.

A waiter came over and smiled, then lifted the Champaign and poured some in each of their glasses. After the waiter left, Jake lifted his glass and smiled at Hanna as she picked up hers.

"To our future," he said and was encouraged by the light in her eyes as she nodded and they tapped each other's glasses lightly and took a sip, as beautiful music played around them.

They looked at the menu and the waitress appeared and took their orders then left.

"This is lovely," Hanna said.

He took her hand. "Yes, you are."

She chuckled. "You are really trying to make my day, I think."

"You have me figured out."

After that they watched people dancing and listened to the music. He wanted to take her out onto the dance floor but needed to wait a bit. The music was romantic and so were the dances. You held your mate in your arms and you danced slowly. He would do that soon but needed the food out of the way first.

Thankfully their food arrived. They ate and

enjoyed each other's company and then when they finished, he asked her to dance.

"I would love to," she said, a gentle smile on her lips.

He led her onto the dance area and pulled her close as the soft, romantic song played. She felt wonderful in his arms and she smiled up at him.

He smiled down at her, wanting to kiss her. "Are you having a wonderful time? I'm having the time of my life with you."

Her expression softened, and her eyes clung to his as her hand in his and her arm around his waist both tightened. "I have never been happier."

He kissed her at last. He had danced them over near the door that led out onto the patio. "Let's go outside for a minute."

He took her hand and led her out onto the patio. It wasn't a patio to dine on, it was a patio with a railing made just for couples to share time together for a few minutes. You could look around and see several couples enjoying each other as they stood out there. He took her to the end of the patio and then, taking her hands in his, he looked into her eyes then dropped down to one knee, still holding her hands.

Hanna's eyes widened. "What?"

"Hanna, would you marry me? If you're not ready yet, I'll stick with you and work with you as long as it takes to convince you. I'm just praying that you're not going to toss me for doing this. I love you with all my heart and I tried to hold off asking you, but I couldn't. I can't imagine another day without you."

Her startled look turned into a huge smile as tears flowed down her cheeks. "Yes, I will marry you. I have been so hoping you would ask me."

Emotion took over and he surged to his feet, picked her up in his arms and held her against him as he kissed her.

She was excited to marry him and he knew he would never ever forget this moment.

Also from Hope Moore

Thank you for reading! Want to be the first to know about exclusive promotions, news, giveaways and new releases? Sign up for my newsletter here: www.subscribepage.com/hopemooresignup

Reviews help other readers find new books. I always appreciate when my readers take time to leave and honest review. It is so helpful to me!

I love hearing from my readers. Please feel free to contact me at authorhopemoore@gmail.com

About the Author

Hope Moore is the pen name of an award-winning author who lives deep in the heart of Texas surrounded by Christian cowboys who give her inspiration for all of her inspirational sweet romances. She loves writing clean & wholesome, swoon worthy romances for all of her fans to enjoy and share with everyone. Her heartwarming, feel good romances are full of humor and heart, and gorgeous cowboys and heroes to love. And the spunky women they fall in love with and live happily-ever-after.

When she isn't writing, she's trying very hard not to cook, since she could live on peanut butter sandwiches, shredded wheat, coffee...and cheesecake why should she cook? She loves writing though and creating new stories is her passion. Though she does love shoes, she's admitted she has an addiction and tries really hard to stay out of shoe stores. She, however, is not addicted to social media and chooses to write instead of surf FB - but she LOVES her readers so she's working on a free novella just for you and if you sign up for her newsletter she will send it to you as soon as its ready! You'll also receive snippets of her adventures, along with special deals, sneak peaks of soon-to-be released books and of course any sales she might be having.

She promises she will not spam you, she hates to be spammed also, so she wouldn't dare do that to people she's crazy about (that means YOU). You can unsubscribe at any time.

Sign up for my newsletter:
www.subscribepage.com/hopemooresignup

I can't wait to hear from you.

Hope Moore~
Always hoping for more love, laughter and reading for you every day of your life!

www.ingramcontent.com/pod-product-compliance
Lightning Source LLC
Chambersburg PA
CBHW070650100726
47907CB00007B/2164